THE KONA STRANGLER

J.E. TRENT

BONUS

Get the free prequel and new release notifications.
https://readerlinks.com/l/965413

1

MAGIC SANDS

MAGIC SANDS BEACH, MONDAY, FEBRUARY 13TH 2012.

Christine Ross was the top producer at the firm she had worked at for the past five years. She was well known and liked in the local real estate community.

She had her ear buds in and was listening to a motivational sales podcast as she jogged along Alii Drive that morning at 5:30 a.m. It was the perfect time to run every morning because there was little traffic and hardly any people out yet. She always wore reflective running shoes that made her easy to spot as she jogged on the side of the road.

Unknown to her was a man working from the top producer's list for the west side of the island that had her name at the top. Christine Ross had the highest gross sales that year on the island and the only way he was going to top her numbers was to kill her.

He had waited for her behind the rock wall next to Alii Drive as she neared the mile marker four sign. It was the perfect place to take her. It was still dark and he had stalked her earlier in the month and knew she always started her week off jogging early in the morning while it was still dark.

He spotted her reflective running shoes in the distance as she approached from the south. When she ran past the four mile marker sign he stepped out from behind the rock wall and grabbed her around the neck with a garrote as if he were roping a calf. Under the cover of darkness he pulled her behind the naupaka growing next to the wall. The garrote cut off the air to her windpipe before she could scream.

He dragged her body from behind the bushes fifty feet down the rocky beach into the water of the small bay. After putting on his fins, mask, and snorkel he had hidden on the beach the night before, he swam Christine Ross' body out a couple hundred yards and let her go.

Earlier that morning he had brought a bucket of chum and carried it out to the rocky point at the edge of the bay and left it there until he needed it. When he swam back to the point after letting go of Christina Ross' body, he dumped the five gallon bucket of chum into the water. His plan was for the sharks to dispose of her body. What he didn't expect was the ocean current that morning to wash her body up on Magic Sands Beach before the sharks could get to her.

Just after sunrise, a jogger running by the beach noticed a body lying in the surf. The waves rolled up onto the sand as if trying to pull the lifeless woman into the sea.

Another competing real estate agent had been removed from the island and now his slice of the pie just got bigger. He didn't need to kill all of his competitors, just the ones who were the most productive.

2

SUNSET CRUISE

Sam fired up the twin diesel engines of the Cabo fishing yacht after everyone was on board. It was a perfect evening for a sunset cruise along the Kona coast.

Sam and Jessica had invited Gabbie to come along for an evening of whale watching as they cruised the Kona Coast. It was the perfect time of year to see the humpback whales that came down every winter from Alaska.

Gabbie was new to the island and was excited to go whale watching again. It would be the first time that Henry had ever gone. Sam and Jessica couldn't wait to see the look on his face the first time he saw a cow and her calf near the boat.

It was about 83° and the trade winds were blowing, which made for the perfect temperature as the boat left Keauhou Bay. The seas were calm and the sky was clear. So clear in fact that Sam said to Jessica, "I bet we see a green flash tonight." Before Jessica could reply, Henry blurted out, "I want to see the green flash!" Jessica smiled and said, "We'll see, honey." Then cut her eyes to Sam, shaking her head.

Sam, Jessica and Henry were sitting on the flying bridge. Gabbie was down below in the fighting chair. She was hoping to catch something for dinner, with the stinger pole they had rigged, as they were leaving the harbor.

Henry crawled up on Sam's lap so he could steer the boat, as Sam explained to Henry how important the rules of the road for a boat captain were. He also kept an eye peeled for the first whale, and Jessica climbed down the ladder to go keep Gabbie company for a bit.

"When I'm out here on the water, the entire world changes," Jessica said. She took a deep breath, filling her lungs with the salty air, and slowly let it out. Gabbie nodded as she kept an eye on the fishing line behind the boat.

"Thar she blows," Sam yelled in his best imitation of a pirate voice as he pointed off the port side of the boat. Henry was jumping up and down in Sam's lap causing him to grimace. He picked Henry up and set him in the chair next to him, to prevent any further damage to his manhood.

Jessica and Gabbie almost fell over the side of the boat from laughing so hard. They quickly turned their attention to the mother and baby whales who had breached the surface in unison near the boat. The looks on both Gabbie and Henry's faces were priceless. They had never seen whales that close before, much less whales that had breached the surface of the ocean, causing a splash twenty feet in the air.

They skirted the pair of whales, heading toward Maui, for twenty minutes before momma and baby disappeared below the surface for good. Minutes later as the sun set on the horizon, they all turned their attention to it to see if there would be a green flash. Sam and Henry swore they saw it. Gabbie and Jessica swore it was their imagination.

Sam turned the boat around to head back toward Keauhou Bay. Gabbie had gone back to sitting in the fighting chair, watching the lure skip across the surface in the boat's wake. Just outside Keauhou Bay, she saw it dip below the surface and heard the fishing reel scream, as yards of line reeled off of it in a matter of seconds.

"You better hope that's not a Marlin," Sam said jokingly. "I don't want to be out here all night." Gabbie didn't pay any attention to him because she was too busy reeling what was about a fifty pound mahi-mahi.

It was only about a fifteen minute fight to get the fish to the boat. It was still light enough to see the translucent gold and green colors just below the surface of the ocean, as the fish came alongside. Sam put the boat in idle and held onto Henry as it rocked heavily back and forth. Once the fish was alongside, Jessica gaffed it and pulled it inside the cockpit and quickly worked to unhook the beautiful fish and get it on ice.

When they got back home that evening, Jessica filleted the fish and they grilled it on the lanai barbecue for dinner. After Gabbie had taken her first bite of fresh mahi-mahi, she said, "That is the best tasting fish I've ever eaten in my life." Sam and Jessica nodded and smiled, as they both filled their mouths with tasty morsels of the catch of the day.

After dinner was over Gabbie said, "Okay, make-believe world is over, I'll see you in the morning." It was the end of a perfect afternoon, and would be the last one like it, for a long time.

3

HONL'S

HONL'S BEACH, FEBRUARY 14TH.

The plan wasn't to strangle Nora Hobbs that evening. She just happened to be a convenient victim and he just happened to hate her guts. Not because she was a top producer; the reason was the deal she had screwed him out of earlier that year–it had cost him a lot of money.

After a long day of driving looky-loos around, showing them property they couldn't afford, he sat in his van eating a plate of barbecue chicken with white rice for dinner, while he watched people come and go from the Sack N Save grocery. When he saw Nora Hobbs walk out of the store all he could think about was giving her the payback that he had promised her someday. He wanted to feel the satisfaction of taking another life again, like how he had felt after strangling Christine Ross. That evening he decided Nora Hobbs was going to fulfill that desire for him.

He watched her put the groceries in the trunk of her car while looking around his van for something he could use as a garrote. It was his favorite tool to kill with. It was quick, quiet, and got the job done without drawing attention; unlike a gun would. "Aah, a power cord should do it," he said to himself, as he reached into the center console to pull one out he used for his laptop computer.

He followed her home. She lived in a small condominium complex on Alii Drive next to Honl's Beach. He pulled into the complex's underground parking lot, after she did, and parked his van right next to her car. It was dark and the nearby light on the garage wall was burned out. Until that point he wasn't sure if he was going to go through with it, but the circumstances were perfect. It was dark and she was alone. And when he scanned the garage, nobody was around.

He drove a Honda van that had an electric door on the passenger side of the vehicle. He flipped the switch to open it as he pulled up next to her car. He came around the back side of the van and met her as she opened her car door. The look on her face was surprise, and then terror, as he wrapped the power cord around her neck and dragged her into his van.

It was one thing to kill a competitor, but strangling Nora Hobbs was a whole different level of satisfaction. It was payback, in its most satisfying form, when he looked into her eyes and said, "I told you you'd pay, bitch," as he watched the last flicker of life in her eyes go dark and she fell limp.

He drove his van out of the underground parking lot onto Alii Drive and thought about the next step. What was he going to do with her body? The solution presented itself within a hundred feet of turning right.

He immediately pulled over next to the two foot high rock wall, in front of the beach park, conveniently located next door to the condo complex. He pressed the button to open the sliding door on his van and looked around to make sure nobody was watching. He then crawled between the seats and pushed her body out the door and over the rock wall onto the grass, and drove away.

"She was found by a surfer," Gabbie said, as she thumbed through the victim's phone looking for her identity, while Jessica looked at the body lying next to the rock wall.

"Strangled," Jessica said, as she studied the bruising on the victim's neck. Gabbie nodded and said, "Nora Hobbs is the name in the settings," as she continued to look at the victim's phone. "The selfie photos match our victim. So it's a safe bet the phone belongs to her."

Jessica nodded, "Another high profile real estate broker. I recognize her name, but not her. I think she uses a photo from twenty years ago in all of her marketing."

While Gabbie was putting the phone into an evidence bag she said, "I noticed that was a common trait here when I was looking for a condo. I'd call an agent and meet with them to see the property for sale and half the time they didn't look anything like their photo online. It always made me wonder about them. You know, if they can't be honest about how they look today, why should I trust anything they say?"

After Jessica and Gabbie finished processing the crime scene, they walked over to the beach and watched the surfers and boogie boarders for a few minutes.

"Why does the one guy have a helmet on?" Gabbie asked.

"There's a reef out there just below the surface of the water. It's broken a lot of surfboards–and heads too, I would imagine," Jessica answered.

They spent the next couple of hours canvassing the condos, next to the beach and across the street, before meeting back in the park.

"I know I must have knocked on fifty doors and had less than ten people answer. The ones that were home hadn't seen or heard anything the night before, or this morning," Gabbie said.

Jessica nodded, "It doesn't surprise me; most of these are vacation rentals that are usually vacant. I had about the same results, except for one old guy that wanted me to come inside for a cup of coffee. But I don't think it was coffee he was really offering," Jessica smirked.

Gabbie glanced over at the second floor of the condos next to the park and saw an old man waving at them from the window–dressed only in his underwear. She grinned and said, "I think the old guy is in love with you."

"Maybe so, but I gave him your phone number," Jessica winked.

After Jessica and Gabbie returned to the task force office, Jessica called her sister, Pua, to ask her what she knew about the previous two victims, since she was a real estate broker and might have been able to shed some light on why someone might have targeted the victims. "I can only tell you two things about them," Pua said. "Everyone loved Christine Ross. And everyone hated Nora Hobbs because she was notorious for shady deals and poaching clients."

4

HAPUNA BEACH

HAPUNA BEACH, ISLAND OF HAWAII, FRIDAY, FEBRUARY 17TH.

He had stalked the woman for a week and watched her swim laps in the ocean off of Hapuna Beach. Her routine every morning started at 6 a.m. She would enter the water at the northern end of the beach, swim out to the rocky point, then turn left and swim south, paralleling the shoreline. Every day was almost the same routine. She would swim four, sometimes five laps.

His plan for her was precise. He was ready as he watched her wade into the sea, just as he had the previous days.

There had been a tropical storm the day before and five to six foot waves rolled into the beach instead of the usual two and three footers. The sun was still behind Mauna Kea; the water had a purple hue as the sun rose.

He watched with anticipation as she waited for the larger sets of waves to subside so she wouldn't get pummeled in the surf.

She quickly swam out past where the waves were breaking, and like the previous mornings, she headed toward the lava rock point at the northern end of the beach. Visibility in the water was poor because of the sand being churned from the ocean floor by the large waves.

He was waiting for her near the point in thirty feet of water. He had two pony bottles of air strapped together that would last about two minutes each; that's all the time he needed.

She didn't see him come up from behind like a shark. The first sign of trouble was when the garrote flashed in front of her face. A second later, her carotid artery slammed shut after he tightened the stainless steel cable wrapped around her neck.

She struggled with both hands to pull the cord away as he tightened the custom-made murder weapon. But it was useless as he pulled her under. She continued to thrash about, she kicked her legs and tried to get free, but ten seconds later she was unconscious. He held the garrote attached to the end of the spear gun tight for another minute until he was sure he had snuffed out the life of another greedy real estate broker for good.

His adrenaline pumped as he removed the cable from her neck after he was certain she was dead. He watched her float free and admired his work as her eyes stared back at him. Every nerve in his body tingled. His head felt as if it would explode in euphoria.

For him, there was no greater experience than to take a life. It had been the third time that week he'd felt the sensation of setting another soul free from the bondage of earth. The urge was no longer dormant, but thirsty for more.

5

BEACH

KAILUA-KONA, FEBRUARY 17TH, 7:05 A.M.

It was the third murder on the Kona side of the island in a week. The first one was at Magic Sands. The second at Honl's Beach Park. The victims were all high profile real estate brokers. Jessica glanced at her phone when she felt it vibrate and saw that Gabbie had texted she was about two minutes away. Thirty minutes earlier dispatch had called them and said there was another victim and to get up to Hapuna Beach ASAP.

Jessica swallowed the last of her coffee, got up from the kitchen table and put the cup in the dishwasher. She glanced over at Sam and Henry. "Gotta go, boys. Have fun fishing." Henry smiled and nodded as he chewed a bite of his waffle. Sam kissed Jessica as she passed by the breakfast table, while heading toward the front door. "Be careful," he said, as he touched her arm.

Gabbie's new 4Runner hadn't arrived at the Toyota dealership yet, and she got stuck driving the ugliest rental car left on the lot. She pulled up in front of Jessica's house in a white Ford Escort with three hubcaps and a dent in the left front fender.

Gabbie rolled down the window and asked, "My car or yours?"

Jessica looked at the car and asked Gabbie, "Are you working undercover on something I don't know about?" while trying to keep from laughing.

"Don't ask."

"Okay, we'll take mine. I want to get out to Hapuna and back as quickly as possible because I have a doctor's appointment later this morning; I don't want to have to reschedule it because your rent-a-pile won't start."

Gabbie followed Jessica into the four-car garage; her mouth dropped open as she gawked at what looked more like an exotic car showroom, and said, "Mercedes, BMW, Ferrari. Yes, please." Then she glanced toward the far side of the garage at the starburst blue '69 Roadrunner. The paint was dull, the hood was flat black and there was a Hooker Headers sticker just behind the driver's side front tire on the lower half of the fender well.

Gabbie wrinkled up her nose and said, "Please don't tell me we're taking that."

Jessica cut her eyes to Gabbie, "'That' will run just a shade over a hundred forty mph in the quarter mile."

"Oh... I detect some hostility," Gabbie snickered.

"No worries, you can relax. We'll take the Ferrari; it's almost as quick and a lot more comfortable. I don't keep the Roadrunner because it's stupid fast or starburst blue. No, it's because my dad and I built that car together when I was a teenager and we'd raced it at the Hilo drag strip. I still like to drive it from time to time, but with over six hundred horsepower and a manual transmission, it's too brutal for a daily driver. And last but not least, climbing through the roll cage to get in was fun as a teenager. Not so much anymore."

Gabbie listened as Jessica reminisced about that time in her life; she could tell by the sparkle in her eyes it was special to her. They climbed into the Ferrari and Jessica backed out of the garage. As the red supercar idled through the neighborhood and the throaty rumble of its V12 bounced off nearby houses, Gabbie sighed as she shifted in the luxurious soft camel colored leather seat that enveloped her body. "Um... I wish I could find me a man that felt this good." Giving them both a good laugh.

After winding their way through Kona town and stopping to get coffee, Jessica pointed the red Ferrari north toward Kohala and set the cruise control for seventy-five mph on the Queen "K" highway. Traffic was light heading out of town since the flow in the morning was people coming into Kona for work.

"Cops in a Ferrari, I almost feel like we're Crockett and Tubbs," Gabbie mused before taking a sip of her coffee.

Jessica laughed. "I was thinking more like Thelma and Louise."

When they hit the two-mile long straightaway before the Waikoloa Resort area, there wasn't a car in sight for a mile so Jessica floored it. The acceleration from the V12 engine pinned her and Gabbie in their seats as the car rocketed from seventy-five to a hundred and thirty mph in seconds.

❧

THERE WAS a cool breeze coming off Mauna Kea that morning. The snow-topped mountain stood majestically in the background of Hapuna Beach. Earlier, a woman in her mid-thirties had washed up on the beach. The sun had risen above the cloud bank and had started to warm the sand. Another perfect day in paradise–except for the dead body.

"Howzit detectives," asked the young policeman as Jessica and Gabbie ducked under the crime scene tape. Jessica nodded as she looked around the perimeter. Gabbie headed straight to the body lying in the wet sand, face down. Jessica turned to Officer Lono and asked him, "Any witnesses?"

"The closest thing we got is one of the beach boys from the hotel who started putting out the lounge chairs on the sand in front. He noticed the victim face down in the surf just before 7 a.m."

Jessica glanced down the beach toward the Hapuna Prince Hotel for a moment and nodded. Officer Lono continued, "We looked for her towel with a bag to see if she had any ID with her but found nothing."

Gabbie kneeled in the sand next to the young woman while she put on her latex gloves. Two minutes later, she motioned for Jessica, who was pretending like she was taking a photo of something in the sand but instead was taking a photo of the crowd gathered on the beach behind the yellow crime scene tape.

Jessica came over and kneeled on the other side of the young woman.

Gabbie lifted the woman's long brown hair off of the back of her neck and motioned to Jessica, "Look at her neck."

Jessica studied the thin ligature mark that circled her throat and sighed, "Strangled." Gabbie nodded in agreement. Jessica looked at the dead woman's face and her brow furrowed, "That's Pam Gorky, she's a real estate agent. I recognize her from her photo, from the real estate section of the Sunday paper. She always had an ad there brokering multimillion dollar homes, if I remember right."

"What's with the one-piece bodysuit she's wearing?" Gabbie asked.

"She was probably training for the 70.3 that is next month."

Gabbie stared at Jessica for a moment. "What's that?"

"It's a half distance triathlon."

After answering Gabbie, Jessica froze as she stared at the tri suit the victim was wearing. A sharp memory from long ago had taken her right back to her youth when a serial killer was preying on female triathletes on the Big Island. It had been years since she'd thought about the murder of her best friend, Malia. It happened during the swim portion of a race they both were competing in back then.

"Are you okay? You look like you've seen a ghost," Gabbie asked.

"I'm okay. This just reminds me about something that happened a long time ago."

"Care to elaborate?"

"This looks eerily similar to the murder of my girlfriend during a triathlon here on the island years ago..."

Jessica continued to look at the woman's swimsuit as she spoke. "I wonder if our guy was in scuba gear waiting for her offshore. He could have grabbed her from below and pulled her under and strangled her with a garrote. Or maybe he used a spear gun with a cord on the end instead of a rubber band. Kinda like what animal control uses to catch dogs. But it looks like he strangled her with whatever he used. Or he held her down long enough to drown her. Either way, we'll know after the autopsy."

"Did they catch the guy that killed your friend?"

Jessica paused before answering, "I thought they did."

After taking more photos and noting details about the scene Jessica and Gabbie drove back to Kona.

"After my appointment I'm going home to switch this car out for something a little more low key and then I'll be back to the task force office."

"Take your time, I'll start working on the murder book."

Thirty minutes later, after driving back to Kona, Jessica dropped Gabbie off. As she drove to her appointment, she wondered what the "twisted piano tuner," as she liked to call the psychiatrist, would want to talk about that day.

6

JESSICA

FEBRUARY 17TH, 11 A.M.

Jessica had been going to her weekly session with the shrink for three months and had made little progress in getting her demons exorcised, as she liked to tell Sam. The doctor wanted her to talk about them and she didn't. Most of the things he wanted to talk about were events she swore she would take to the grave, much less tell another living soul.

Who she really wanted to talk to was Sid Akiona. He was part of the investigation of the murder of her girlfriend Malia, back when Jessica was still a teenager. Sid was a responding officer when one of the serial killers tried to take Jessica out, too. He had recently retired from the force and Jessica didn't have his phone number. But she remembered Uncle Jack had taken him fishing a few times as payback for when Sid had helped them out in a situation a couple years back.

Jessica called Uncle Jack as she drove home from the Mexican standoff she had with the shrink.

"Hey Uncle, do you have Sid Akiona's number handy?"

"I think so, hang on."

"I'm driving, just hang up and text it to me if you don't mind."

"Sure kid, I got to get back to washing the boat."

Uncle Jack was never one for long conversations on the phone. It probably had something to do with why he still lived alone on his boat. Sure enough, the text came through a minute later and Jessica clicked the phone number link to make the call. It rang twice before Sid answered.

"Howzit Sid, its Jessica Kealoha."

The first thing out of his mouth was, "Have you got rid of that billionaire boyfriend yet?"

She laughed, "Not yet, but you'll be the first to know when I do," she teased.

"Oh well. What's up Jessica?"

"I need to talk with you about an old case with Dieter and Hans Schilling. Dieter was the guy who offed my...," Sid interrupted, "I remember, what do you want to know?"

"Do you think there were more killers working together than just Dieter and Hans?"

Sid paused for a second, "At the time I thought there might be a third killer working with them but couldn't find any positive evidence to support that."

"What did you find that caused you to think there might be a third killer?" Jessica asked.

"We found a third set of fingerprints on some of the souvenirs they had taken from the victims. The prints didn't match any of the victims or Dieter and Hans. That's why I always suspected there might be a third killer. In the years following there weren't any more murders other than the usual one or two a year. So I came to believe the two Schilling brothers were the only killers working together. Is this related to the task force you're working on? I heard about it through the wireless coconut."

"Maybe, maybe not. We had another victim this morning, and it looked like the murder took place while she was training for the upcoming triathlon. She washed up on

Hapuna Beach. It became obvious it wasn't a drowning by the ligature mark around her neck."

"Is it possible she got caught in a fishing net and drowned before she could get free of it?" Sid asked.

"No, we didn't find any signs of a net on the body."

She thanked him for his hypothesis and got off the phone with a promise to stop by and talk story sometime.

❧

JESSICA RETURNED HOME and Mr. Jangles greeted her at the front door when she swung it open. He was a huge Maine Coon cat that weighed eighteen pounds. He had been mistaken for a bobcat more than once by the neighbors, even though bobcats weren't indigenous to Hawaii.

She had never been a cat person, but accepted Mr. Jangles as part of the deal of living with Sam. She had grown to like the big fur ball more than she thought she ever would, since she had always considered herself more of a dog lover.

After setting down her purse, she got the big kitty untangled from between her legs and went into the kitchen to check his food bowl.

Jessica glanced at the red light blinking on the answering machine on the counter inside the doorway of the kitchen. She pushed the play button while opening a fresh can of cat food and had to listen carefully to hear the message over the sound of the electric can opener. She stopped the noisy machine for a second until she heard it was Pua and then restarted it while continuing to listen to the message.*"Hey Jess, there's a party tonight. I know it's short notice but my biggest client is hosting it out at Kukio and I need a wingman. I'll be there to pick you up at 6 p.m."*

Jessica felt a wave of anxiety shoot through her gut; it was the last thing she wanted to do. But she thought it might go a long way in helping rebuild her relationship with her sister, since they had struggled to get along over the years. Besides, she needed a short break to give her brain a rest from all of the stress of the day's events.

She had no excuse to stay home since Sam and Henry were fishing at South Point and wouldn't be home until the next afternoon. And it would be nice to get out of the house for a girl's night out for a change.

The thought of going to a social function full of people she didn't know was one of her greatest fears and secrets in life. It was unknown by anyone who knew her, not even her sisters Pua and Jasmine. Nor had she told Sam, but thought he would figure it out eventually on his own. No need to share all of her secrets with him upfront, she thought.

As a homicide detective in L.A. for over twenty years, she had no social anxiety when on the job. Carrying a gun and a badge will do that for you. But the anxiety in her private life had been periodically debilitating. When invited to a social event like a party, where she didn't know anyone, she just about broke out in hives thinking about having to go. It baffled her that she couldn't figure out why the fear in her personal life was so overwhelming sometimes.

❧

AS 6 P.M. APPROACHED, Jessica was touching up her lip gloss when she heard Pua talking loudly on her phone as she walked in the front door of the house. She hurried to finish and told Mr. Jangles, "Be a good boy and guard the house," as she went out the front door with Pua.

The sisters got into Pua's new BMW parked in the driveway.

Her younger sister glanced over and sneered at the plain white Chevy Malibu Jessica had bought recently.

"Geez, why don't you drive a BMW or something European? It's not like you and Sam don't have the cars," Pua said as she touched up her torch red lipstick in the rearview mirror.

"Does the air of superiority come with it, or do you have to pay extra for it?" Jessica fired back without missing a beat.

The sisters couldn't be more opposite in some ways. Besides their choice in cars, outward appearance was one of them. When it came to making an entrance, Pua's weapons of choice were a little black dress and Christian Louboutin red sole pumps. Jessica was more of a sneakers, tee-shirt, and Levi's kind of gal but could dress to the nines if going out with Sam to an important business dinner. That evening Jessica wore a sundress with a hibiscus print and sandals.

On the drive out to the Kukio Resort, Bruno Mars blared through the BMW's sound system. The sisters were getting in the party mood as they sung along to the music while they cruised down the highway. The sun was setting; the sky was a majestic red with hues of purple and streaks of yellow crossing the Kona coast. Jessica thought for a moment if there was a god, and he painted the sky, that's what it would look like.

Going to this party with Pua would be a test for her nerves. She had been taking a new antidepressant for the last six weeks and felt as close to being whatever "normal" was for the first time in her life. That medication was also the first thing that had worked besides alcohol when it came to coping with the social anxiety that had been giving her fits since she was a young child.

But with booze, it eventually had started doing "to" her instead of "for" her, which led to getting sober or getting fired. It was her choice according to her boss at the time.

They arrived at Kukio just as other guests were starting to pour into the clubhouse where the party was being held. Before getting out of the car Jessica was going to tell Pua about Pam Gorky's murder and said, "Hold on a sec." Pua had her door open and one foot out of the car; she stopped and swiveled back toward Jessica. "We had a... never mind. I'll tell you about it later." Jessica changed her mind and decided to wait until after the party to let Pua know a real estate broker had been murdered that morning at Hapuna Beach.

7

KUKIO PARTY

EVENING OF FEBRUARY 17TH .

The party looked like the who's who of the Big Island. "I've never seen so many Tommy Bahama shirts," Jessica whispered to Pua as they entered the clubhouse pavilion.

Besides anxiety, the other thing Jessica hated about going to social functions on the island was the likelihood of running into someone she'd rather not see. And this party was no exception. Larry Black was there, hobnobbing with the captains of industry. It didn't take long before he spotted Jessica across the room and started working his way through the crowd toward her.

She and Pua were chatting with Ron Ford, a well-known real estate broker and principal of Kona Connections. Pua had done a few deals with him over the years and liked Ron because he was one of the straight shooters on the island who was a real pro and an all-around good human being, too. It was a lot more than she could say about most of her colleagues.

Pua and Ron were commiserating about the new reality of selling property in the twenty-first century when Larry inserted himself in the conversation. "You have to learn the technology just enough to be able to hire someone else to handle it." Ron and Pua nodded. Jessica just glared at Larry, hoping he'd be like a bee and buzz off.

Larry ignored the stink eye from Jessica and asked, "Where's Sam? I'm surprised he'd let you come to a party alone."

Jessica shot back, "He doesn't 'let me' do anything. I do what I want. Oh, by the way, how's that federal investigation coming along?"

It was Larry's turn for the hard looks as he walked away without saying another word.

"What was that all about?" Pua asked as Ron excused himself to go chat with another broker.

Jessica leaned in close and whispered, "The FBI's been knee deep in Larry's ass since they found out he's involved up to his eyeballs with the Russian mob."

Pua acted like she was surprised to hear it, but there had been whispers throughout the real estate community for years about Larry's dealings. She nodded, and looked over Jessica's shoulder as she waved to a potential billionaire boyfriend she'd been stalking for some time. "Excuse me for a couple of minutes; I have to go talk to him."

The last thing Pua wanted to talk about was any dealings with the Russians and her real estate business, since she too had done a couple of deals with them on multimillion dollar properties. Jessica understood that because Sam was selling yachts to Larry's mob clients. So everyone had skeletons in the closet when it came to doing business with Larry Black and the Russians.

Jessica's worst fear of standing in the room alone had come true after Pua went to talk to Mr. Big Bucks. For a split second she wished she could have a shot of tequila to take the edge off, but that bus had left the station in her life and she just had to figure out a different way to cope with the anxiety.

As Jessica tried to be a wallflower, Pua came stomping

back and said, "Why didn't you tell me they found Pam Gorky murdered this morning at Hapuna?"

"I started to when we were getting out of the car but changed my mind, thinking I didn't want to upset you before going into the party. I wasn't sure how well you knew her, so I decided to wait. I'm sorry."

Pua didn't say anything, but Jessica could see the sadness in her face. "I take it you were friends?" Pua's eyes welled up with tears. "We paddled together last season. We even did the Molokai race together. She was a good person. Who would want to kill her? What the hell is wrong with people?"

Her sister's reaction took Jessica aback. Pua almost always kept her emotions close to the vest. "Let's go. I'll tell you what I know on the way home," Jessica said as she put her arm over Pua's shoulder and walked her toward the door of the clubhouse.

Jessica motioned for Pua to hand her the car keys since she hadn't been drinking at the party and Pua obliged. It was a clear night, as they drove back to Kona, and the sky sparkled with stars. This time the stereo was off and the mood somber.

"Remember years ago when my girlfriend Malia was murdered during the triathlon race?" Jessica said.

Pua nodded she did and Jessica continued, "I always thought there was only two killers. But now I'm starting to wonder if there might have been a third."

"Why's that?" Pua asked.

"Because of where and how Pam was killed. When I saw her on the beach this morning, it all came back. Pam was attacked offshore while she was swimming, just like Malia." Jessica paused for a moment because, even years later, the thought of Malia being taken in such a violent way still bothered her and now was not the time for her to get emotional when she had to be strong for Pua.

"I don't want to scare you, but I want you to pay attention to your surroundings; I know you're always careful, but you need to be vigilant until we find the guy responsible for Pam's death. There's other victims too that might be the work of the same killer. I told you I was going back to work for the Kona PD, but that's not entirely accurate. I'm working on a task force put together to find the guy we think is responsible for Pam's death and other victims throughout the state."

"Is he targeting only real estate agents?" Pua asked, her brow furrowed.

"We think so. I can't say too much about it right now, but what I can say is there have been five real estate agents murdered statewide, Pam was the sixth. After the second one in a week, the tourism authority and the mayor demanded the Governor provide funding to set up a task force to find the killer. Since the Island of Hawaii has had the most victims, this is where the task force was chosen to be headquartered."

"I didn't hear about them because I don't watch the news or read the paper; it's always such a downer all the time. I've heard a couple of rumors from other agents, but I didn't take them seriously because I don't have time for that stuff. I just ignored them and kept my nose to the grindstone, but now I'm starting to think I should be concerned," Pua said.

"Chances of him targeting you I think are pretty slim. But like I said, be alert to your surroundings. And it probably wouldn't be a bad idea to get back into the dojo to sharpen your skills. Did you ever take the test for a black belt?"

"No. I'm still a brown belt. But it's been a long time since I've practiced Kempo. Maybe you're right. If nothing else, it would be good to get back into it. Maybe we could go together like the old days."

8

TASK FORCE OFFICE

SATURDAY, FEBRUARY 18TH.

It jolted Jessica awake. It was dark; she rolled over and stared at the clock until her eyes could focus. After her eyes adjusted to the darkness, she saw it was 5 a.m. She breathed a sigh of relief that it was only a nightmare. But her next thought was *not this one again.*

This particular nightmare was no stranger to her; it had haunted her for years after Malia's murder. She couldn't remember the last time she'd had it, other than it being at least fifteen years or more since it startled her awake.

She thought about the recurrence of the nightmare as she listened to the rhythms of the waves crashing against the rocky shoreline across Keauhou Bay. The sound of the ocean drifting through the open bedroom window calmed her nerves. Her nightmare was a twisted version of what had really happened over twenty years ago. In the dream, she was always responsible for her friend's death.

But the truth was there had been nothing she could've done to stop Dieter Shilling from firing the stainless steel spear from his spear gun into Malia's chest that morning when they were racing to the turnaround buoy during the triathlon. Intellectually, she knew it wasn't her fault. But somewhere in the dark reaches of her mind there was always that thought, maybe she could have somehow prevented it.

Jessica had enjoyed thinking about that nightmare all she could stand and got up to go turn on the coffee pot. While the coffee brewed, she got in the shower. She stood under the warm spray and let it beat down on her shoulders and exhaled deeply, letting all the stress of the nightmare wash away.

She got dressed, grabbed her 9mm out of the gun safe in the nightstand and went to the kitchen. The aroma of the Kona coffee filled the room. She picked up her favorite mug sitting next to the pot and filled it. It was one of those cups that when anything hot like coffee was in it, a photo of Sam and Henry became visible on the side of the mug. She missed them even though they had only been away from home one night and hoped they were having a good time fishing down at South Point.

A glimmer of sunlight started to break through the darkness as she sat in her favorite chair on the lanai and stared at Keauhou Bay while sipping her coffee. By the time she had finished, it was daybreak, and the birds chirped to announce the start of another day. She watched as a canoe with a women's crew paddled by; it reminded her of Pua and Pam Gorky paddling together. It also reminded her it was time to go to work.

She went into the kitchen and poured another cup of coffee for the drive to work. She enjoyed driving her plain Jane Chevy Malibu because she never had to worry about anybody running into it or door dings in the parking lot. A Jack Johnson CD was playing Banana Pancakes, and it made her wish she had a plate of them for breakfast. Her stomach growled as she listened to the song while she cruised Alii Drive along the coast toward Kailua town.

The surf was dropping in height by the hour as the tropical storm earlier in the week got further away from the island. It was three to five feet, and the surfers had packed Lyman's Bay to get as much surfing in as possible before the swell died down.

She stopped the car in the parking lot across from the bay and backed into the only empty parking space left so she could watch the surfers while she sipped her coffee. It looked just like it did every winter, for as long as she could remember; pickup trucks with construction racks and surfboards filling almost every available parking spot on days with big surf.

There would be many people late for work that day because anytime the waves were big, a lot of them wouldn't show up for work on time. Or, maybe they skipped work altogether.

Jessica watched the surfers ripping up and down the waves, some of them riding almost all the way into the rocky shoreline and others bailing out of the wave early and getting back in the lineup. As the sun rose over Mt. Hualalai, the ocean had a pink glow from the reflection of the sun off of the clouds that were skirting the coast. If there was a heaven, that's what it would look like, she thought.

After she swallowed the last sip of coffee, she started the car and pulled slowly back onto Alii Drive and detoured to the donut shop in town before going to the new task force office. Gabbie sat at her desk, working on the murder book and reviewing cold case files, when Jessica walked in and handed her a fudge brownie and a cup of coffee. "Life is short, eat your cake first. Or in this case, your brownie," she said.

"You got that right," Gabbie agreed as she smiled and reached for her treat.

Gabbie took a bite of the fudge brownie just before Jessica asked her, "Anything interesting in there?" Gabbie nodded her head, as she chewed the brownie and swallowed it so she could answer.

"There's a lot of missing persons reports that were never closed. Most of them are young women on the Hilo side of the island going back almost twenty years."

Jessica's brow furrowed as she stood looking out the window at the ocean as a sailboat passed by. She slowly chewed her malasada and thought about what Gabbie had just said.

"I wonder if we have two different guys hunting women," Jessica said.

Gabbie nodded again in agreement. "One guy doesn't leave a trace of the victims and the other is like a cat, he wants his kill on full display."

9

O'HALLERAN

SATURDAY, FEBRUARY 18TH.

Grady O'Halleran had been a detective with the Honolulu Police Department for over twenty-five years and was known as a hard ass who got the job done. His younger colleagues considered him a dinosaur. He had a smart phone he hated, a wife he hated more, and he drank like a fish–both on and off the job.

O'Halleran was a lot of things, but crooked wasn't one of them. And since the Honolulu Chief of Police was crooked as a dog's hind leg, he was more than happy to approve the governor's request of sending O'Halleran to the Big Island.

He was handpicked by the new governor to be in charge of the special task force because he had closed more murder cases in Hawaii than any other detective.

O'Halleran was sixty-three years old, set in his ways, and he wasn't crazy about working with women detectives. But that was the hand he was dealt and he would make the best of it since he only had two years to go before he could retire and do what he really liked to do, which was sit on his boat and drink beer.

A serial killer in Honolulu had managed to evade capture, and O'Halleran wasn't sure if the killer had pulled up stakes and moved to one of the other islands to escape the manhunt on Oahu. But he damned sure wanted to find out before he retired. And since bodies were starting to pile up on the Big Island, he thought it was as good a place to start as any.

And besides, his wife said there was no way in hell she was moving to Kona. It was the perfect excuse for him to get away from her for a while. He wanted to divorce her, but he didn't want to give her half his pension, so it was cheaper to keep her. And an assignment on an outer island was just what the doctor ordered. That and a gin and tonic.

When he arrived in Kona and walked into the new task force office for the first time, he thought he'd really stepped in it this time. The office was intentionally set up away from the police station so the day-to-day operation at the station wouldn't be a distraction to the task force. That didn't bother him. It was the size that he didn't like. Much too small compared to where he had just come from.

The office was on Walua Road, not far from the center of town. It was on the second floor, had a view of the ocean and it was about six hundred square feet all together, including the bathroom. But they didn't need a lot of space since the "task force" comprised only three detectives. At least that was what O'Halleran was told by the powers that be.

The new office was more like a closet that he, Jessica and Gabbie would have to work out of. There were three desks in the center of the small room and a couple of large white-boards on the wall. It could work; besides, it was about a hundred and seventy-five miles from his wife, which seemed to be just about right to him. In the big picture it was the lesser of two evils.

❧

THE DAY after Pam Gorky was murdered, O'Halleran was pacing back and forth in the task force office, while on the phone, listening to the governor complain about the mayor who was complaining about the chief of police in Hilo not doing enough to help find the killer.

"Yes sir, we will find this guy." O'Halleran hung up the phone just as Jessica and Gabbie walked into the office for the first time. After they introduced themselves and shook hands, he eyeballed Jessica and Gabbie to size them up, as they did to him.

Jessica had worked robbery homicide in Hollywood before retiring and moving to the Big Island, and Gabbie had retired from the FBI. He had read their files, and both said they were good cops. But everyone looks good on paper, he thought. Well, except that detective over in Hilo that was too stupid to replace the coke he had stolen out of the evidence room with baking soda. No wonder they had a serial killer roaming the island with impunity, he thought.

O'Halleran spoke first. "Let me get this straight; you guys were both retired, and you willingly came back on the job?"

Jessica and Gabbie nodded and Jessica said, "Gabbie and I worked together previously in LA and we work well together, we trust each other to have our backs. Everyone knows the Kona PD is understaffed and could use the help. We wouldn't be able to sleep knowing we have a predator stalking us. So, here we are. The sooner we find this guy, the sooner we can get back to lying on the beach."

"I can respect that," O'Halleran said as he looked Jessica and Gabbie in the eyes; he felt good about what he saw looking back.

He continued, "There's been talk all over the state that there might be a serial killer hunting women here, Maui and Oahu. And I would probably add Kauai to that since they've had a couple of mysterious murders too."

Gabbie looked at Jessica and said, "I have a question; is it too late to move back to the mainland?"

Jessica ignored her and looked at O'Halleran. "She hit her head on the way over here. She's fine, don't worry."

O'Halleran wanted to laugh but kept a stiff upper lip and barely cracked a smile.

"The governor, mayor, and chief of police will be here later this afternoon for a pow-wow. We'll meet them over at the civic center conference room at 2 p.m."

Meeting the upper echelon to play twenty questions was the last thing Jessica and Gabbie wanted to do right then. The clock was ticking and they needed to get to work to find the killer before he struck again.

The sigh of relief was clear on both of their faces when O'Halleran said, "Don't worry, I'll keep the brass off your ass. Because like you guys, I had requirements too when I took this job. One of them was they would leave us the hell alone so we could do our jobs and I'll remind them if I have to."

O'Halleran's phone rang, and it was the secretary at the governor's office. "Okay, thanks for the call." He clicked the off button on his phone and set it down on the desk he'd been leaning against during the whole conversation.

"Good news. No meeting today. They've postponed it until later in the week."

10

REPORTER

SATURDAY, FEBRUARY 18TH.

Jessica's cell phone rang; she glanced at the number and didn't recognize it. It was a mainland number; probably a telemarketer, so she let it go to voicemail. A minute later she noticed the message icon on her phone light up. She tapped the speaker playback button to listen to it.

"Hi, I got your name from a friend at the police station and he said you're the detective I need to talk to concerning the murder of Pam Gorky."

Jessica straightened up in her chair, grabbed her pen and rested it over a legal pad sitting on her desk.

"I'm Danica Bradshaw, a new reporter here at the Kona Herald. In today's mail I received a large envelope containing a couple of documents related to the murder of Pam Gorky. You'll want to see them and the demand it makes. We can meet at Lava Java or I can bring it to you."

Jessica tapped the call back button on her phone and Danica picked up on the first ring. "Aloha, this is Danica."

"Howzit, this is detective Jessica Kealoha."

"Oh hi. I have a large envelope you're going to want to take possession of. It was addressed to me; the sender must have gotten my name off of a story byline. I opened it and it says if the paper doesn't print the enclosed manifesto another real estate agent will be killed and he will keep killing them until the paper prints it."

"Where and when can we meet?" Jessica asked.

Danica replied, "Lava Java in thirty minutes, OK?"

Jessica agreed to the time and place and said she'd see Danica shortly. Gabbie had gone to the police station to get more cold case files. Jessica texted her to drop what she was doing and meet her at Lava Java ASAP.

❧

DANICA BRADSHAW WAS EARLY for the meeting with Jessica. She was fresh off the jet from the mainland and out to make a name for herself at the Kona Herald. She was wearing a business suit, heels, and looked like she was on her way to anchor the six o'clock evening news.

Jessica spotted her waiting out front of Lava Java holding a large vanilla envelope and approached her.

"Danica?" "Jessica?" They both shook hands and Jessica introduced her to Gabbie.

Danica gave Jessica the letter which briefly said exactly what Danica had told her on the phone. If the newspaper didn't print the killer's manifesto, he would resume killing real estate agents until they did.

"Apparently he's really pissed off about real estate agents," Jessica said, as she scanned the letter and then handed it to Gabbie.

Danica interjected, "This Sunday it will be a page one story. And most likely a series of follow-up stories after that. Unless–"

Jessica finished Danica's sentence, "We agree to give you the inside story first."

Danika smiled.

"Here's what's going to happen," Jessica said. "I will call

your publisher when I get back to my office and ask him to please publish the whole batshit crazy manifesto. Even if I have to personally pay for it."

The smile on Danika's face evaporated and Gabbie reached her gloved hand out for the envelope that Danica was still holding, and she reluctantly handed it over.

Danica's eyes narrowed as she clenched her teeth. But she didn't say anything at first, then blurted out, "Don't I get some credit for calling you?"

"Girl has a point," Gabbie said to Jessica.

"You're right Gabbie, she does."

"Here's a suggestion Danica, you're new here in town right?"

"Yes, that's right," she answered.

Jessica looked up and down Danica's suit. "Ditch the suit for something more casual that doesn't scream you're fresh off the jet. Don't play games with us and we'll hook you up with the story first when we can."

Danica's brow relaxed and she looked open to the advice.

"Kona is like a lot of small towns on the mainland," Jessica said, "you scratch my back and I'll scratch yours. That will get you a long way here on the island."

Danica's expression showed she agreed, and she nodded. They shook hands and left in opposite directions.

Jessica and Gabbie were walking back to their cars when Jessica turned and said, "She could be an asset if we raise her right."

Gabbie smiled at her partner. "I'll scan all the documents in the envelope and then I'll get the originals shipped off to the FBI crime lab in Quantico. Hopefully, Danica didn't pass them around the newsroom for everyone to read before calling you. Otherwise, it's going to look like DNA soup."

Jessica nodded and sighed.

11

SUNDAY PAPER

SUNDAY, THE 19TH.

The publisher of the Kona Herald did what Jessica asked and published the killer's manifesto on the front page of the Sunday edition. It was a rambling diatribe about real estate agents and developers being scumbags. The killer viewed them as being responsible for the destruction of sacred lands on the island and he was just doing his part to clean up riffraff from the island.

It was about 10 a.m. as Jessica sat in her favorite chair on the lanai sipping coffee while watching the tour boat across the bay load passengers. A few minutes before, Mr. Jangles had been running around the lanai doing his best to catch a gecko. He wasn't having any luck with the lizard, so he gave up and came and sat next to Jessica. He stared at her until she got the message to scratch him behind the ears.

While she scratched his right ear, she glanced at a text from Sam earlier that she had missed. It said he and Henry were extending their fishing trip and wouldn't be home until the next day.

As she stared at the turquoise blue bay behind their home and daydreamed, her phone jolted her when it rang. It was O'Halleran. It must be important, she thought when she saw it was him calling her on a Sunday. "What's up?" she said.

"The mayor wants a meeting tomorrow. He's foaming at the mouth because of the front page article in the Kona Herald with the serial killer's manifesto they printed this morning. He said his phone has been ringing off the hook with calls from real estate brokers demanding the police do something right away to catch the killer."

"It doesn't surprise me. I figured a lot of feathers would get ruffled when the paper printed the manifesto. But if it keeps the whacko from killing any more people, I think it's a small price to pay."

"Agreed. I just thought you'd like an early heads up since you're invited to the party tomorrow with the mayor, and because the article mentioned your name."

"Okay, I'll be there." Jessica clicked the button on her phone to end the call. She thought about her life with Henry and Sam, and how she was missing them. Maybe, after she and Gabbie caught the serial killer, she would retire again. Maybe.

She didn't mind the job; it was the politics of it she had no appetite for anymore. Not that she ever had before, but her nonsense tolerance was almost zero at this stage in her life. Maybe she and Gabbie would open their own private investigation… and again her phone rang, jolting her out of thought. This time it was Pua.

"Good morning, sis," Jessica said while reaching for her coffee cup on the table next to her lounge chair.

"What's so good about it? I just read the paper. You guys have to find that lunatic."

"Yes, that seems to be the current theme this morning," Jessica replied.

"How can you be so flippant about it?" Pua said.

"I'm sorry. If it's any consolation, the mayor will most likely be reaming me out over this tomorrow."

While initially upset, Pua calmed down after expressing her displeasure about the murderer running around the island scot-free.

"We're waiting for the results from the FBI. Maybe they'll get lucky and find fingerprints or DNA on the evidence we sent them."

"How long until you hear something?"

"Hopefully in the next week. And a word of advice. Try not to be alone out in public until we catch this guy."

"I can't believe it's come to this. I miss the old days when Kona was a kinder, simpler place," Pua said.

"Me too. Just be careful," Jessica said.

"Always. I got to go, I have a house to show."

12

MEETING & UNCLE JACK

MONDAY, FEBRUARY 20TH.

It was 2:15 p.m. when Mayor Davis and his entourage arrived at the civic center. When they walked in the door to the meeting room he was complaining to one of his underlings about the president of the Island Real Estate Brokers Association calling him, demanding they catch the killer sooner than later. And the Tourism Authority was clamoring for an end to the situation by any and all means necessary.

Word of a serial killer was starting to get a lot of traction on mainland news outlets like CNN and Fox News. There was even a rumor that Dateline would soon come to the Big Island to film an episode.

Gabbie was running down leads and didn't have to attend the meeting. So it was Jessica and O'Halleran on one side of the conference table and everyone else on the other. The mayor started with, "Who thought publishing the manifesto from a whack job was a good idea?"

O'Halleran defended the decision when Jessica interjected, "I did."

"On whose authority?" the mayor questioned.

"I asked her to ask the Herald to run the manifesto," O'Halleran said. Jessica didn't ask him to take up for her, but she was glad to see he stepped up to defend her. The mayor gave O'Halleran a dirty look and paused for a moment to listen to an aide who was whispering something in his ear.

"Detective Kealoha, what's the plan, since you're quoted in the paper as asking the publisher to post the manifesto?" the mayor asked.

"I think that question is better suited for Detective O'Halleran."

"I'm not asking him, I'm asking you," he said in an angry tone of voice.

Jessica took a deep breath in through her nose and exhaled slowly, giving herself a five second buffer before responding and saying something she'd regret.

"The plan is to catch this guy. But I am curious. During the short time this task force has been working we've discovered there's about fifteen cold case disappearances all over the island going back almost twenty years. They were all women who society ignored: homeless, runaways, prostitutes. And nobody seemed to care about them being missing. What's up with that?"

The mayor glared at Jessica and said, "This meeting's over."

"Well, that went well," O'Halleran said to Jessica as they walked out of the meeting. Jessica nodded and said, "I'll see you back at the office after lunch." O'Halleran nodded, and they got in their cars and left the West Hawaii Civic Center. O'Halleran took the new highway from the civic center and Jessica drove down the Queen "K" back to town. She needed to talk to Uncle Jack at the harbor.

***

Uncle Jack was doing what he liked to do best when Jessica parked in front of the slip of the *A Hui Hou*. He was sitting in the fighting chair at the rear of the boat, reading the paper and smoking a cigar. Jessica could see he was in his element when she walked up the dock toward the boat.

"Hey kid, what's going on?" Uncle asked.

"You know I'm over forty, right?" Jessica asked, somewhat annoyed.

"When you get some gray hair I'll quit calling you kid. You don't look so happy, what's going on?"

Jessica sat on the transom, at the rear of the boat, facing Uncle Jack and asked him, "Do you remember the murder of my girlfriend Malia years ago?" Uncle nodded he did as he took a puff off his cigar.

"Everyone thought there were only two killers. I have a bad feeling there might have been a third one that got away. We had a murder victim wash up on Hapuna Beach, and I don't have any evidence yet to prove it, but the MO was similar to how Dieter Schilling killed Malia. But instead of a spear gun, the killer used a garrote of some kind from the look of the bruising on the victim's neck. Maybe I'm reading more into this because the victim was training for the upcoming triathlon."

Uncle Jack nodded and said, "Interesting, you'd think the third one, if there was a third one, would have continued on killing. But I'm no expert in serial killers."

Jessica nodded and said, "Maybe he did. There's a lot of unresolved missing persons reports of women across the island over the last fifteen years or so. Maybe he's decided to ramp back up now and become very public about it."

"You might be right. Time and evidence will tell. I was reading the nut job's manifesto in the paper earlier today when I was having my morning coffee. You know, he will have some supporters. A lot of people hate real estate agents."

"I know. Speaking of coffee, do you have any?"

"It's in the galley, help yourself, but you'll have to make it."

Jessica stood up and started toward the galley and asked, "Do you want some?"

Uncle Jack shook his head no. "It's five o'clock somewhere," he said, and reached into the small cooler under his chair and pulled out a bottle of beer, then followed Jessica into the galley to show her where the coffee filters were.

He pulled out a big bag of Starbucks beans, handed it to her and pointed to the coffee grinder. She gave him the side eye for a moment for not having Kona coffee, but didn't say anything.

"What can I say, at Costco it's cheap, and it's good."

They sat at the dining table while the coffee was brewing. Uncle Jack cracked open his beer and took a swig and said, "If you ever start drinking again, this is good stuff." He turned the bottle so she could see the label of the locally brewed beer that had become very popular.

"Doubtful," she said, as she glanced over at the coffee pot to see how it was coming.

"In another minute or two it'll be ready. I have the fastest coffee pot on the island. I love that thing," Uncle Jack said when she looked toward the pot.

Just like he said, a minute later she was pouring herself a cup of black magic. "I have to get one of these pots, ours is slow as molasses." She took a seat on the couch across from Uncle Jack. She positioned herself near the air-conditioning vent to cool off. She wasn't sure if she was getting hot flashes or it was because the trade winds had stopped blowing that day and it was muggy.

"Are you ready to retire again after being back on the job?" Uncle Jack asked.

"No. Not yet. But if I have to deal with the politics of it being a high profile case, I might. The head of the task force is a guy named O'Halleran. He's from the Honolulu PD. Have you ever heard of him?"

Uncle Jack shook his head.

"He seems like a stand-up guy. But everyone knows the Honolulu PD has a lot of rotten eggs in their basket. I'd just like a little insight into who I'm working with, that's all."

After Uncle Jack took a swig of his beer he said, "I'll reach out to a detective over there who was our liaison with NCIS and see what he says."

"Do you miss the job?" Jessica asked.

"Sometimes. But it's good to just go fishing when I want too. I'll check out your new boss and let you know if there's anything to worry about."

Jessica nodded, gave Uncle Jack a hug and went to meet Gabbie for lunch.

***

Gabbie had arrived ten minutes earlier and already put their order in before Jessica got there. As Jessica walked to the table where Gabbie sat, she glanced at Kailua Bay across the street from the popular eatery. The normally calm bay had three foot swells topped with whitecaps. The wind was blowing from the south. Jessica took a deep breath in through her nose and said, "Smells like it will rain soon."

"How did your guys' meeting with the mayor go?" Gabbie asked just before picking up her iced tea to take a sip.

"It was short. I brought up the fact you found a lot of cold case reports that have never been closed, and the mayor got his panties in a snit and ended the meeting."

Gabbie raise an eyebrow, "Just like that?"

Jessica nodded and moved her water glass to the side of the table as the waitress approached with their Cobb salad.

"It was weird; I guess I struck a nerve with him."

After Gabbie scooped half of the salad onto her side plate, she said, "I've gathered all of the cold case DNA to compare to the recent murders."

Jessica nodded and replied, "It'll be interesting to see what turns up. But I still think whoever's strangling the real estate agents is a different guy."

13

KUKIO VICTIM

MONDAY, THE 20TH.

Sam and Henry had returned from their fishing trip to South Point, and Jessica could smell the fish cooking when she walked in the front door. Sam had many good qualities about him, but the one Jessica liked the most was the fact that he liked to cook and he was good at it. She could hear his voice in the kitchen, patiently explaining to Henry how he was doing things as he prepared the fish.

She almost didn't want to interrupt them because it sounded like such a special time of bonding between the two. When Sam stopped talking for a minute, it seemed like a good time for her to announce that she was home, and she gave Sam a kiss and Henry a hug.

It wasn't long until dinner was ready and they all sat down at the table in the dining room overlooking Keauhou Bay.

"How was your day?" Sam asked.

Jessica smiled and answered Sam's question with a question.

"Did you guys catch lots of fish?"

"Henry was the big fisherman. He caught a mahi-mahi and a couple of ono."

Jessica looked at Henry who was grinning from ear to ear as he chewed a bite of the ono he had caught.

She had just taken her third bite of mahi-mahi when her cell phone started buzzing in her pocket. She pulled it out and looked at the screen. It was Grady O'Halleran.

"Excuse me boys, I have to take this." Jessica got up from the table and went into the living room.

"What's up, Grady?"

"There's been another murder. I'll text you and Gabbie the address."

Jessica apologized to Sam and Henry for having to leave in the middle of dinner. She kissed them both goodbye. "I'll be home as soon as I can."

As she walked to the garage she thought about Sam's pupils for a moment and how they looked constricted at the dinner table. It was only a passing thought and she decided she'd probably been to too many courses on how to spot people under the influence and figured she was just being paranoid.

***

This time she took her Malibu, picked up Gabbie and they drove out to the Kukio Resort, just as the sun was setting off of the Kona coast.

It always mystified her as to why an island that was so beautiful could have things happen there that were so ugly.

She and Gabbie pulled up to the guard shack at the entrance to the multimillion dollar Kukio community. She showed her badge to the guard who opened the gate and waved them through.

They were going to a beachfront home where the murder occurred. She knew this would be a super high-profile case. Whoever owned the home would likely have equally high-level connections in the business world, and politically, too.

Gabbie was looking at all the houses as they passed by on

the way toward the beach. "There are video cameras all over this place," she said.

Jessica answered, "Security is super tight because there are more billionaires with homes in this community than anywhere else in Hawaii. This is where the richest of the rich live. Otherwise known as the one percent. The truth is, most of them don't actually stay here full time. They have houses that they visit two or three weeks out of the year. Most of the people, who own massive computer companies, own homes in Kukio. Dell, Gates, and a few hedge fund managers to round it out. Almost all are billionaires. A lot of the people that live here could have bumper stickers on their car that would say my other car is a jet."

"Why don't you and Sam have a home here," Gabbie asked.

"We like our place in town better. Our boat's parked right outside. These guys have to go back down the highway to the harbor if they have a boat," Jessica said, as they parked behind a police 4Runner with its glowing blue light on top.

***

Jessica went to talk to Mark Taylor, who was the first officer on the scene. He said the victim's wife came home from shopping in town and found her husband dead. "The victim's name is John Lancaster; he's a real estate developer."

"Where is she?" Jessica asked.

"She went to the neighbor's house across the street."

Jessica thanked Officer Taylor and walked to the neighbor's house to talk with Mrs. Lancaster.

A man opened the door after Jessica rang the doorbell. She identified herself and asked to see Mrs. Lancaster.

It was not who she was expecting to see when the young woman came to the door. She was blonde, mid-twenties with an hourglass figure, and wearing a mini-skirt that looked like it had been spray painted on. And she didn't look like she had shed one tear over her husband's death. Since Mr.

Lancaster was easily old enough to be her father, Jessica was in full skeptic mode as to who was responsible for his murder.

Just like the last time, Gabbie went straight to the body. The victim was sitting in a recliner like he was watching TV, except someone had strangled him. There was no sign of a struggle. The only telling evidence was the wide red line around his throat.

After Jessica interviewed the wife, she walked back across the street to the crime scene. She and Gabbie stood there looking at the dead guy. "You just can't make deals with serial killers like you used to," Gabbie said.

"I'm not so sure about that yet," Jessica said, her brow wrinkled.

14

SWIMMING PUA

Jessica started swimming at the pier five days a week after joining the task force, so she could burn off the stress of the job. She usually went after work or during lunch time.

She loved to swim to the old Hilton and back. It was almost like meditating. She could be in her own head, but not really there, all at the same time.

Another thing she loved about swimming from the pier was that sometimes she would come across dolphins. That was as close to a spiritual experience as she had ever had in her life. On the days she didn't feel like swimming, she thought about the dolphins, and willed herself to go to the pier. She was always glad she had when she'd reached the second buoy.

By the time she got to the fourth buoy, she always thought about the time she found Malia dead there with a spear in her chest. As the serial killer investigation went on, she thought about it every time she got to the fourth buoy. Sometimes the memory was sharp, and other times it was like a ghost in passing. The good thing about crying in the water was nobody would notice.

On the days Gabbie joined her, they would only go to the fourth buoy and back until Gabbie could swim a longer distance. On one such day, Jessica had coaxed her to swim far enough past the fourth buoy that they were in front of the the Kona Inn, before they stopped to turn around.

They treaded water there, for a few minutes, to rest while taking in the view of the palm trees swaying in the wind in front of the old inn. Jessica shared a bit of the history of the inn, which was the first resort in Kona. How it came to be as a result of the steamships visiting the island in the early part of the twentieth century.

"I'm telling you, if this detective thing doesn't work out, you should be a tour guide," Gabbie joked, just as a small wave hit her in the face, filling her mouth with saltwater, causing her to choke momentarily.

Jessica laughed, "Are you ready to head back?" Gabbie nodded and they started swimming toward the pier. They had gone a couple hundred yards when Gabbie stopped and yelled, "I have a cramp in my leg!"

Jessica was busy looking at a huge school of trumpet fish, twenty feet below her, and didn't hear Gabbie. She had continued swimming for another fifty feet when she noticed Gabbie wasn't beside her.

When she stopped and looked back, all she saw was the top of Gabbie's head, as she was sinking below the surface, while trying to rub the cramp out of her leg.

Jessica spun around and swam back to Gabbie, kicking her fins and pulling each stroke in the water as hard as she could. When she reached Gabbie, she showed her how to get rid of the cramp by grabbing the tip of her swim fin and pulling on it to stretch out the leg muscles.

Gabbie did exactly as Jessica showed her and within thirty seconds the cramp was gone. They continued back to the pier, this time with Gabbie in front.

By the time they got back to the sandy spit of beach next

to the pier, Gabbie was exhausted and lay down in the sand to catch her breath. She had never swum that far before; it was both terrifying and exhilarating all at the same time.

After they had rinsed off, they went to the coffee shop next to the banyan tree and got a couple of cappuccinos to warm their core after the long swim.

"Now I see why you swim here all the time," Gabbie said as she held the warm cup of liquid between her hands. "The fish I saw were amazing. It was like swimming in an aquarium."

Jessica nodded, "I love swimming this time of year because you can hear the whales too."

"I heard them," Gabbie said. Then her face went from looking excited to serious. "They won't eat us will they?"

Jessica laughed, "No, they won't eat us. But the tiger sharks are a different story."

15

VALENTINE

TUESDAY, THE 28TH.

A week later, the results from the FBI crime lab came back. They had found a fingerprint on the manifesto that belonged to a man named Clarence Valentine. When Jessica and Gabbie looked into his background, all they could find was that he'd been arrested once for failing to pay a speeding ticket that he'd forgotten about.

"You think this is our guy?" Gabbie asked, sitting at her desk across from Jessica.

"Too early to say. Let's find him and see what he has to say."

Gabbie nodded.

Clarence Valentine was easy to find since he owned an auto repair shop in town and listed it as his occupation on the warrant in his previous arrest.

Valentine's Auto Repair was in the old industrial area of Kona, in a building that set back off of Alapa Street.

Jessica and Gabbie parked outside the office door to the shop and a man in a white shirt, holding a clipboard, came out. He looked puzzled as to why their car was in front of the shop, since according to the shop's schedule there wasn't supposed to be any Malibus coming in that week.

"We're looking for Mr. Valentine," Jessica said.

Before the service advisor could say another word, Jessica held up her badge. The man pointed over toward the far corner of the shop and said, "He's under the car over there. I wouldn't go talk to him right now; he's pretty mad about something."

"We'll take our chances. Thanks."

Jessica and Gabbie looked around the shop as they approached the lift where Valentine was sitting on a stool working underneath a car hoisted overhead. "Be careful not to step in that," Jessica said to Gabbie as they walked through the shop. There was coolant and oil puddled all over the floor. The shop was a pigsty compared to the wheel alignment shop down the street where Jessica had taken her dad's Roadrunner recently.

"Mr. Valentine, we need a word."

"Make an appointment," he said in an angry tone of voice while still looking up at the car's engine from underneath the hoist."

"We're detectives with the Kona PD."

That got his attention. He dropped the wrench he was holding, and it made a loud tinny sound as it bounced off the concrete floor and echoed through the shop.

"We want to know how your fingerprint got on a document sent to the Kona Herald. To be exact, the document was the manifesto printed on the front page a week ago. The anonymous author was someone who said they were responsible for Pam Gorky's death and there would be more to come if they ignored his demands."

"I want a lawyer," was Valentine's only response.

"Stand up and put your hands behind your back Mr. Valentine," Jessica said.

While Gabbie was putting the cuffs on him, she said to Jessica, "We're not putting a greasy mechanic in my new 4Runner."

Jessica nodded and read Valentine his rights while Gabbie radioed dispatch asking for a transport vehicle to pick up the suspect.

Twenty minutes later, a marked blue and white Tahoe pulled up to take Valentine to the Kona police station.

It didn't take long for the coconut wireless to spread word around town that a suspect was in custody for the murder of Pam Gorky.

Jessica and Gabbie returned to the task force office to inform O'Halleran they took Valentine into custody.

"He lawyered up right from the get-go," Jessica said to O'Halleran.

Gabbie shook her head and said, "We didn't even get a chance to play good cop, bad cop."

"Do we have anything more than the fingerprint on the manifesto?" O'Halleran asked.

Jessica sighed, "No."

O'Halleran said, "I'll call the district attorney's office so they can send someone over in the morning. When this guy's lawyer shows up, we'll see if the DA wants to charge him."

***

As Jessica drove home that evening her phone rang and it was Uncle Jack. He said, "I heard back from my contact in the Honolulu PD. He said O'Halleran is a good detective, but he drinks like a fish. Other than that, you don't have anything to worry about."

She thanked Uncle Jack for following up and got off the phone. Having spent a number of years on the job with alcohol in her bloodstream during working hours, she was the last one to throw stones when it came to that, just as long as he could do his job.

16

ANGELA REYES

WEDNESDAY, THE 29TH.

Clarence Valentine wasn't the smartest guy in town by far. But he was smart enough to call a well-known criminal defense lawyer in Honolulu by the name of Angela Reyes. He knew her name from all the press coverage she got in high-profile cases on Oahu. She had represented clients who everyone thought was guilty, and she almost always got them off.

When he called Ms. Reyes from the Kona jail, she gave him the same advice she gave all of her clients, "Keep your mouth shut and do not under any circumstances say one word to anyone until I can fly over in the morning."

The next morning Angela Reyes stepped out of her Lincoln Town Car in front of the Kona police station. The crime level in Kona had grown so much over the past couple of years, she kept the car in the airport parking lot to save time. Lately she was flying over an average of once a week to represent clients on the Kona side of the Big Island.

Ms. Reyes met with Clarence Valentine before her meeting with the deputy DA assigned to the case. At least that's what she thought would happen. Most of the time the deputy DA was an underling, fresh out of law school. Not that time. That day the big boss, Carrie King from Hilo, was there in person.

Ms. King was the Hawaii County District Attorney, and she started with, "We have your client's fingerprint on the manifesto he mailed to the Kona Herald."

Valentine's attorney countered with, "He hates real estate agents. That's not a crime. Yes, he made a threat. Charge him with terroristic threatening. But he did not murder any of those real estate agents or Pam Gorky. And he was only blowing off steam with empty threats if his manifesto didn't get printed. He'll be happy to plead to a terroristic threatening charge. But that's it."

"Why would your client send a manifesto, like he did, to the newspaper?" the DA asked.

"Like I said, because he hates real estate agents. He says the reason he hates them is because of all the appointments they didn't show up for to get their cars repaired at his place of business. He owns an auto repair shop. And they never called to cancel or let him know that they would not make it to their appointments. As a class, he feels they are the worst customers on planet Earth."

King crossed her arms as she listened. Her body language said she wasn't buying it. But Reyes didn't let up and continued. "The time he got jerked around selling his house compounded this. Agents promising to show up at a designated time and never doing so. Never calling to let him know, or to apologize for the six hours he spent cleaning his house, before each showing, for nothing. That's why the guy hates real estate agents, because most of them are flakes. His words, not mine."

Ms. Reyes could see the wheels spinning in Carrie King's head when she added, "We both know the guy you're looking for isn't dumb enough to leave fingerprints on anything. And, Valentine has an alibi for the day of Pam Gorky's murder."

The DA's brow furrowed, and she said, "Let's hear it."

"He was in Honolulu at a strip club the day of the murder and has the credit card receipts to prove it."

District Attorney King threw her pen down on the conference table, sat back in her chair and exhaled loudly.

"Okay."

***

Before she headed back to the airport, Angela Reyes collected a check from Clarence Valentine for a retainer of five thousand dollars plus travel expenses, for 30 minutes' worth of work with the DA and the upcoming hearing she would have to attend. "Not bad," she said out loud, as she patted her purse and smiled.

The DA charged him with terroristic threatening in the 1st degree and Valentine posted bail that day.

17

SHOP

FRIDAY, MARCH 2ND.

Ulrich Schilling was at Lava Java having his morning coffee when he read the manifesto from the Sunday paper.

The thought of someone taking credit for his work was unacceptable to him, and there would have to be consequences for Clarence Valentine.

Daisy Carvalho arrived early for an appointment to get her car fixed that morning. When she walked into the office of Valentine's Auto Repair, Clarence was sitting behind the desk in his office–dead as a doornail. Someone had strangled him. He looked like he had put up a fight for a moment because his ashtray was on the floor, and papers from the top of his desk were strewn all over. When Daisy stopped screaming she called 911. The police arrived in about three minutes since the shop was around the corner from a donut shop.

"We have another one," O'Halleran said, on the phone.

"Okay, I'm on my way," Jessica replied. She kissed Sam on the lips and headed to what was starting to be the daily murder.

Jessica and Gabbie pulled up in front of Valentine's shop and parked the car. There were half a dozen police cars in the lot. And Danica Bradshaw was already there, too. It was a regular zoo. The first responding officers did a good job securing the crime scene and keeping people out of the office.

This time Gabbie went to interview the responding first officer on the scene. And Jessica went to look at the body in the office, which was off to the side of the shop. The medical examiner's van was blocking the front entrance so Jessica went through the shop to the side entrance of the office.

She was careful as she walked across the shop floor not to step in the antifreeze pooled in spots on the floor. She thought to herself, "How does a guy work in such a dump?"

She leaned down and was looking at the bruise around Valentine's neck. It was thin just like all the others, except for Langston's, which was wide. And again, it looked like a garrote was used to strangle him.

Gabbie walked over and said, "I guess he was telling the truth that he really wasn't the serial killer."

18

BONNIE JAMES

TWO WEEKS LATER. FRIDAY, MARCH 16TH.

The award for the real estate broker of the year in West Hawaii was going to Bonnie James. She was getting ready for the awards dinner that evening at a gathering of her peers out at the Hilton.

She worked at a large firm that had expanded recently from the mainland; though the firm was new to the island, Bonnie wasn't. She had lived in Kona a long time and had become known for specializing in ocean front properties. She spent her mornings surfing up and down the coast and knew which shoreline houses got flooded during big storms and which ones didn't. That expertise had positioned her as *the* oceanfront property expert on the Kona side of the island. As a result, she had closed more oceanfront sales than any other agent on the island that year.

Besides selling real estate all over West Hawaii, Bonnie was a part-time high-end escort. Her special website had a list of gifts men could bring to her and the wine she preferred. Since Kona was a small town, she blurred her photos on her website so no one would recognize her out in public and, with the exception of a couple locals, she had a policy of only dating visitors from the mainland, who could afford the finer things in life, since her rate was twelve hundred dollars an hour.

She had worked hard that year in her real estate business because she knew the clock was ticking and her highest paid years as an escort were almost over. She was thirty-seven years old and soon she would either have to drop her rates or quit the escort business and focus on real estate full time. The latter was the choice she made when she learned she had won the broker of the year award.

None of her co-workers at the firm she worked at during the day knew about her part-time gig at night, turning tricks to supplement her income. Or so she thought. She knew a couple of the girls she worked with had worked the pole in a Honolulu strip club before going into real estate. So who were they to judge her, even if they had found out?

As Bonnie looked in the mirror and touched up her ruby red lipstick, she smiled. Her plan was working. The next thing she wanted was a man with big money and power. Soon she'd have that too. Her mama always said, "Use what God gave you, Bonnie!" She smiled at her reflection when she thought about it one more time before leaving for the awards banquet.

Later that evening in the ballroom at the Waikoloa Hilton she stood there smiling at her peers, applauding her achievement. She knew she was well on her way to the success she craved after years of struggle. She had clawed her way up through the ranks from selling coffee shacks to multimillion dollar estates.

In 2009 when the real estate market came to a screeching halt, she started her escort service and at three hundred dollars a pop she entertained nameless johns visiting the island on vacation who were looking for a good time. She was willing to do whatever it took so she could keep a roof over her head.

She finally had the validation she needed. Her peers

would present her a diamond pendant that evening as her symbolic key into selling the most expensive real estate on the Big Island. Now was her time to reel in the big ones and only broker properties priced at a minimum of a million dollars plus–and give up the escort business for good.

The previous year's winner of the broker of the year award came up on stage and presented Bonnie with the coveted ruby and diamond encrusted pendant that the annual winner always received. Over two hundred and fifty people were clapping and smiling back at Bonnie as the former winner pinned the pendant on her dress. Except for one guy in the front row, who sat there with his arms crossed and a blank look on his face.

While he sat in the midst of the audience, his anger boiled as he watched Bonnie James strut up to the stage to receive the award that should have been his. He watched in disbelief as they chose her over him. He grossed more sales that year than she. He sold the most expensive property on the island; he closed the most transactions overall. There wasn't any doubt in his mind they rigged the award to Bonnie, and he couldn't let go the injustice of it.

He had heard the rumors about her part-time business as an escort. He laid out a simple plan on his way home from the Hilton. He sent an email to what he was sure was Bonnie's website and said he wanted to make an appointment as soon as possible for an overnight date.

The overnight rate listed on her website was nine thousand dollars. On her way home, Bonnie saw the email, forwarded to her phone from her website, letting her know she had a potential client.

When she read the client wanted an overnight gig, she couldn't resist the temptation and decided she'd do one last date and use the nine grand to buy something nice for herself as a reward for all of her hard work. Usually she never made a date without twenty-four hours notice; but she was in a good mood that evening and decided to make an exception.

She emailed him back and asked how soon he wanted to meet. His response was less than five minutes later when he replied, *"Tonight if possible."*

She answered, *"Last minute will cost you an extra thousand,"* not caring if he said yes. She was on a roll and would go out of the escort business with a bang. Bonnie gave him instructions to her private condo that she used only for her escort business and told him she would only take cash.

He texted her back, *"No problem, I have it in the safe in my hotel room and I'll bring it with me."*

Bonnie didn't follow standard procedure that night, and it would cost her. She always checked out her clients before their first date. But it was getting late, and she was on her cell phone while driving back to Kona from Waikoloa. She skipped checking him out since he would be her last client ever. She just wanted to get it over with and go shopping the next day.

19

MOONLIGHT

FRIDAY, MARCH 16TH.

It was a perfect evening; the moon was out and the sky was clear. The moonlight reflected off of the ocean like a giant flashlight shining for miles across the sea. The surf was light, and it was quiet, with only the sound of the ocean lapping against the rocky shoreline in front of Bonnie's condo.

It didn't take her long to get ready before her client would arrive. All she had to do to was get changed into something more comfortable. She removed the diamond pendant and put it in a small jewelry box on top of her dresser in the bedroom.

When the buzzer rang at the gate, she was ready for him. She had on a black teddy and garter belt with coffee-colored stockings that had the line going up the back of them and stiletto heels. When she greeted him at the door at the bottom of the staircase, she wore a red silk robe.

The client had gone to great effort to conceal his identity, and she didn't recognize him. When he arrived, he was wearing a long-haired blonde wig with sunglasses even though it was dark outside. She invited him in and asked, "What would you like to drink? I have gin, wine, and whiskey." She always started her overnight sessions getting to know each other a little before getting down to business, and a little alcohol was the perfect lubricant to use for a new client.

After an awkward silence he answered, "I'll have the gin with tonic if you have it."

"Got it," she said, as she reached into the refrigerator to get the tonic water. She detected he had a German accent but didn't say anything; she decided it would be something to use as a conversation starter once the drinks were ready.

He sat on the couch in the living room that overlooked the ocean and tried not to look at her while she was in the kitchen making drinks. Bonnie James was a real Miss America and not staring at her beauty took a lot of effort.

She had her back to him in the kitchen as she poured the gin into a glass with two ice cubes. It would be a shame, he thought. She had long legs, and he loved the dark line going up the middle of the back of her stockings. He hadn't seen that in a long time, and it was very arousing.

He could see she was almost finished making the drinks. He got up and walked to the bar that separated the kitchen from the living room. He pulled ten grand out of his satchel and put it on the counter. It was a single bundle of hundred-dollar bills, tightly wrapped with the band on them from the bank. After laying the money down, he turned around to stare at the ocean. Bonnie had glanced toward him while fixing her drink and saw he had put the money on top of the counter. "Thank you," she said. "Here you go," as she sat his drink up on the bar. She then picked up the money and put it in a drawer, in the kitchen, that had a lock on it with a keypad. She smiled as she punched in the required four numbers to open the safe. With the money tucked away, she turned once again to her guest.

He took a sip and set the glass back on the bar. "Excellent. Thank you."

"Is your accent German?" She asked.

He nodded and said, "Yes, you're right."

Bonnie had poured herself a shot of tequila, after downing it and a bit of small talk she asked him, "Would you like to start in here first, or the bedroom?" A lot of the men she had dated in the past liked to have sex while looking at her and the ocean through the open sliding glass doors. She always kept them open, so the ocean breezes kept the condo cool and created an ambience for her clients.

Like most of the others, he said he wanted to start in the living room. She took off the silk robe and draped it over the couch that was off to the side. He watched her like a wolf would watch its prey. But she'd never make it to the bedroom.

20

SECRETS

MARCH 19TH.

O'Halleran called Jessica and Gabbie and told them they had another victim and to meet him at the Hale Kona Kai condominiums off of Alii Dr. When he got the call from dispatch he was practically on scene since he lived down the street in a small apartment overlooking Lyman's Bay and had gone home for lunch.

Twenty minutes later, Jessica and Gabbie rolled up at almost the same time, a minute apart. Bonnie James' cleaning lady was sitting at the bottom of the staircase leading to the condo. She was a middle-aged Filipino named Mahalia Aquino who had worked for Bonnie the last year and a half.

She had her head in her hands and her eyes were puffy from crying when Jessica and Gabbie walked up. She moved aside and pointed up the stairs. Jessica and Gabbie both lightly touched Mahalia's shoulder as they passed by her.

When they entered the condo, Bonnie was face down and naked in the center of the living room. O'Halleran knelt down on one knee, looking at her face turned to the side.

He looked up at them and said, "Cleaning lady found the body when she came to clean the condo. By the looks of the bruise around her neck, it looks like she got strangled. Her name's Bonnie James, according to the housekeeper. Do you guys recognize her from the real estate signs up and down Alii Drive?"

Jessica and Gabbie both took a good look at the victim's face and nodded in agreement. Gabbie said, "She looks just like the photo on the sign except for the grey skin from being really dead for a while. Jessica and O'Halleran gave Gabbie the side eye but didn't say anything.

Just like the previous victims, it looked like a garrote had been used to strangle her. There were no signs of a struggle. Death had been fast, just like the others. Whatever kind of cord the killer had used squeezed closed Bonnie's carotid artery in seconds, and she was unconscious in less than twenty. If she struggled, it would have been even sooner before losing consciousness.

Gabbie went to talk to the neighbors to see if anybody heard or saw anything, out of the ordinary, over the last couple of days while Jessica examined the body.

When she returned, Jessica motioned her over to look at the long fingernails on Bonnie's left hand. "She took a swipe at whoever killed her, and got some skin underneath her nails," Jessica said.

Gabbie nodded and said, "Hopefully our killer's DNA comes up in the database."

"Did you get anything from the neighbors?" Jessica asked.

Gabbie shook her head and replied, "None of them had ever seen or heard the victim. A couple of them said they'd seen lights on here from time to time in the evening, but they hadn't seen anyone coming or going."

Bonnie James' condo was an end unit. The dual sliding glass doors facing the ocean provided a million dollar view, and there was an exterior window on the same side of the living room as the outside staircase. Jessica caught a glimpse of Danica Bradshaw and her photographer out of the side window and muttered to Gabbie, "What the hell is she doing here?" Gabbie walked to the window to look and said, "Apparently, that wireless coconut you've mentioned before is getting faster–or the police scanner." Jessica shook her head and said, "She's the last thing I want to see right now."

The two patrolmen posted at the bottom of the staircase wouldn't let Danica Bradshaw anywhere near the crime scene upstairs. She asked one of them to at least ask Detective Kealoha for a minute of her time and that it was important. One cop asked her how she knew Kealoha was upstairs. "I saw her looking at me through the window," she said.

"Okay, hang on," the older cop replied. He obliged and went upstairs to relay the message while the younger cop made sure Bradshaw had no ideas of following.

Jessica came down the stairs a few minutes later and asked Danica, "What's so important?"

"I was supposed to meet Bonnie James here for an interview today. Is she okay? Two nights ago she was awarded the Hawaii Real Estate Broker of the Year award at the Hilton. It was a big event with agents from all over the islands attending. I even brought a photographer with me for the story. She was going to show us the ruby and diamond pendant that she received," Danica said.

"Pendant?" Jessica questioned.

"Yes, it's supposed to look like the Big Island. You didn't answer my question. Is she okay?" Danica said.

Jessica shook her head. "No. She's dead. Call me tomorrow and I'll try to give you more." Jessica handed Danica her card and went back upstairs to the crime scene.

O'Halleran was on his phone and Gabbie was sketching the living room and taking notes of everything she saw when Jessica came back in the room.

"Did anybody see a ruby and diamond pendant anywhere in here?" Jessica asked.

Both O'Halleran and Gabbie shook their heads.

Jessica relayed the information she had gotten from

Danica Bradshaw and the three of them went to work searching the condo looking for the pendant, besides other clues. In the middle of the search the medical examiner showed up. After he was there for a while, Jessica came out of the back bedroom to ask him some questions. "How long do you think she's been dead? And what do you think caused the bruises on the outside of her butt cheeks?"

"Based on the color of her skin and there is no rigor mortis, I'd say she's been dead at least forty-eight hours. My guess is she was having sex with whoever strangled her. He must have been slapping her on the rear with both hands."

"I have just one more question. Do you see anything that would lead you to believe the killer had sex with her after she was dead?"

The medical examiner shook his head and went back to writing on his clipboard.

Jessica thanked him and started toward the back bedroom to go through it one more time, looking for the pendant, when Gabbie, who was in the kitchen said, "This is weird." She had been looking through all the drawers except for one that was locked. "Have you ever seen a drawer in the kitchen that had a commercial keypad lock on it like this?"

Jessica came around the end of the bar to see what Gabbie was talking about.

"Nope. You're right, that is odd. It looks like something that should be on the front door. I'll call the locksmith."

O'Halleran returned from searching the bathroom and they all stood in the kitchen looking at all the empty drawers. The only thing in the kitchen besides one cabinet full of booze was a corkscrew remover and a couple of empty glasses in the sink. No plates. No silverware. No food. Nothing. The refrigerator had a couple cartons of orange juice and that was it.

The whole place was weird; there was minimal furniture. The closet in the bedroom was empty, except for a single dress on a hanger that Bonnie had hung there when she'd changed for her client.

There was a king size bed, but it only had a sheet on it and a couple of pillows. Opposite the bed was a dresser with a big mirror and an empty jewelry box on top of it. The dresser top drawer was full of lingerie that looked like it all came from Frederick's of Hollywood. The second drawer was full of sex toys and bondage wear. The remaining drawers of the dresser were empty.

The locksmith was running behind because there were a lot of tourists who locked their keys in the car that day. Ninety minutes later he arrived at the Hale Kona Kai condominiums. By the time he showed up, the medical examiner had already left and transported the body to the morgue.

The locksmith had the drawer open in less than five minutes. Gabbie, Jessica, and O'Halleran stood behind him while waiting for him to leave, after he had picked the cylinder lock in the handle, so they could see the contents of the drawer. The locksmith wasn't the slightest bit curious about what was inside, like they were. He left quickly for his next appointment. It was a tourist who had locked himself out of his rental car at the beach and was calling him every fifteen minutes, complaining about how their vacation was being ruined because he was taking so long.

"You saw it first Gabbie, you open it," Jessica said.

Unlike when Geraldo Rivera opened the safe on live TV, there was something in the drawer. Gabbie's eyebrows raised, and she said, "I can't remember the last time I saw ten grand anywhere but at a drug bust,"

"I know someone in vice I need to go talk with about this," O'Halleran said.

21

SHRINK

TUESDAY, MARCH 20TH.

Jessica's eyes opened. They took longer than normal to focus because of a lack of sleep; it had been a long night of tossing and turning. The nightmare was back in full force and she had slept only a couple hours the whole night. When she rolled over, Sam was leaning on one elbow looking at her. "Good morning, beautiful," he said.

"Liar," she whispered. "But keep it up."

"That's my job," he replied as he leaned over to kiss her on the forehead.

She looked at the clock on the nightstand behind Sam, realized she had overslept, and jumped out of bed to go make Henry's breakfast.

Before she got to the bedroom door Sam said, "Relax, I already took care of Henry. He's on his second bowl of cereal right now. Auntie May is on the way over to pick him up. She's going to take him out to Aloha Village. She's teaching all the kids how to string flower leis today."

Jessica stopped mid-stride and turned around. "Thank you. I know I haven't been home a lot because of the case. That ends when we catch the guy we're looking for. Once he's in jail, I'm re-retiring. I promise."

Sam met her in the middle of the room and they embraced for the first time in the past week. "Don't worry, honey. Just do what you do best so we can get back to normal and nobody has to worry about a psychopath on the loose roaming the island."

After Jessica kissed Sam and Henry goodbye, she left the house and drove along Alii Drive toward Kailua town. She liked to play Hawaiian music every morning as she drove along the coast. She always played Slack Key Guitar Masters Volume One when she wanted to sooth her nerves. Since Pam Gorky's murder, her nerves had been tighter than a guitar string. Between the recurring nightmares and the lingering thoughts in the back of her mind, that there was a third serial killer involved in Malia's death that escaped justice, the only way she would have any peace was to find the killer.

On the way into town, she stopped at Dr. Williams' for an early morning appointment before going to the task force office. In her previous sessions with him, she hadn't wanted to take part any more than she had to. That was because she was at a level of discomfort that was tolerable and she thought she could live with the skeletons in her closet. The only reason she was seeing a psychiatrist was to keep Sam happy.

She had known for a long time that something wasn't right with her, but now it had come to a head, and she would have to deal with it if she ever wanted a good night's sleep again. The nightmares had become intolerable.

Frequently she'd wake up in the middle of the night from the recurring nightmares. Sometimes she lay there for hours afterward thinking about the similarities of Malia's and Pam Gorky's murder. There was no evidence to support what she felt in her gut. But she felt it and had learned a long time ago to always listen to her instincts.

Jessica wasn't crazy about sharing her innermost secrets

with the shrink. She was always painstaking in what she said to him during their sessions. She was a firm believer that the only way to have a true secret was that only one person on the whole planet knew what that secret was. There were some things in her past that she just had to take to the grave. One of them could cause her to lose her job and possibly even go to jail.

But on this particular visit, she would open the door to most of the skeletons in her closet. She had no choice; she wasn't sleeping, and it was affecting her ability to think. And she wouldn't be able to think straight enough to catch a serial killer if she didn't start getting some sleep soon.

When she walked into the office of Dr. Williams, he was standing next to the coffeepot in the corner of his small waiting room mixing a concoction of sugar and cream into his coffee cup. He looked up when he heard the door open and saw it was Jessica and said, "Good morning, coffee's ready if you'd like some." She nodded and replied, "Good morning, I'll just take a straight IV in the left arm, please," as she headed to the pot.

It had been a month since Jessica's last appointment. After Dr. Williams had taken a sip of coffee to make sure his coffee tasted just right, he looked up and glanced at the bags under her eyes.

With coffee in hand, she followed him into the private room where they always had their sessions. It was a comfortable room with a view of the ocean from the couch where she always sat. Through the open window she could hear the surf splashing along the shoreline less than a hundred yards away. It was still early, and it sounded like hundreds of birds chirping in the two massive banyan trees outside the window.

Dr. Williams' chair was partially in the room's corner and pointed toward the couch where Jessica sat across from him.

After shuffling papers on his desk for a moment, he sat down in his leather chair across from her. He crossed his legs and rested his hand into the side of his face as he reviewed his notes from their last session. A minute later when he looked up at her he studied her face again and said, "You look exhausted, anything in particular you would like to discuss this morning?"

She nodded her head just before taking a sip of coffee. She paused for a moment before continuing. "I haven't been sleeping well. I keep having a recurring nightmare." She explained the dream and how she felt responsible for the death of her friend Malia years ago. Jessica spent the entire hour pouring her guts out about what had happened to her best friend back then and how that had prompted her to go into police work when she was old enough to attend the academy.

Dr. Williams sat in his chair and listened while taking notes. Toward the end of the session he told her his recommendation was that she be willing to do some work and that he thought he might be able to help her.

"What I want you to do is start writing about it. What it will do is empty the poison out of your subconscious. I want you to write down everything about it that makes you angry and/or afraid. I want you to do this every day for at least 15 minutes. Bring the paper with you on your next visit and we'll discuss it. It won't fix you in a week. But you have to start somewhere and writing about it is what I want you to do first."

"I don't have time for that right now. I have to find a serial killer who's strangling real estate agents to the tune of once a week right now."

"Do the best you can. If you can't write fifteen minutes, try to write for ten. If that does not work, try five. Eventually, five will become ten, and ten will become fifteen. I promise if you try, it will work."

Jessica frowned and nodded she'd at least entertain the thought of trying to write every day. She wasn't crazy about digging up monsters out of her subconscious since she was trying to find a real-life one. But she had no choice. It was that or die. And dying wasn't an option because she was responsible for Henry now.

22

TASK FORCE

TUESDAY, MARCH 20TH.

When Jessica walked into the task force office, Gabbie was working on the murder book. "Did I miss anything?" she asked.

"No, O'Halleran was here and left. He said he was going over to the station to talk to an old colleague from Honolulu that's now with the Kona vice squad."

Jessica went to work looking through Bonnie's social media profiles online, and in less than an hour she had found a photo of the pendant they had awarded her for being the top producer on the island. "This has got to be it according to the timestamp on Facebook. It looks like Bonnie had posted this photo on the night of the murder during the awards ceremony. Take a look, Gabbie."

Gabbie got up from her desk and came around to Jessica's so she could see the photo. Bonnie had taken a selfie at the awards ceremony while she was wearing the ruby and diamond pendant, and tagged the location so there wasn't any doubt of the time and place.

"I don't know if the pendant is significant. Maybe she put it somewhere else before her murder. Or the killer stole it. But

I can see this seems to really bug you," Gabbie said and returned to her desk.

Jessica didn't reply to Gabbie; instead she turned her chair halfway around to look out the window. A sailboat cruising by just off of the shoreline caught her attention while she tapped the top of her desk with her index finger. She turned back toward Gabbie and said, "Collecting souvenirs was one thing the guy that murdered my friend Malia did. When we catch this guy, it won't surprise me if we find a stash of souvenirs taken from all the other victims. Years ago, the guy that murdered my friend was collecting jewelry from his victims. He and his brother, who was his murder partner, had both taken souvenirs from most of the women they killed."

Jessica and Gabbie heard a loud stomping on the stairs outside their office. "Sounds like we have company," Gabbie said. The door opened, and it was O'Halleran. "What was that noise we heard when you were coming up the stairs?" Jessica asked.

"That was me stomping the shit out of a centipede. Geez, I hate those things. I got some good intel over at the PD. I talked to my buddy in the vice squad. I'll tell you all about what he said, but first I have to use the head."

"That sounds interesting," Gabbie said. Jessica continued where she left off when O'Halleran walked in. "Until this time there hasn't been a sexual element to the murders. Most of these serial killers have sex hang-ups. I don't think our guy has a kink he needs to feed because he didn't rape any of the other victims."

Gabbie replied, "Why would he have sex with the last victim only. What makes her different?"

O'Halleran had come back out of the bathroom and interjected, "Besides being a real estate broker, she was a hooker."

Jessica held up her index finger to O'Halleran to wait a second while she opened a drawer on the side of her desk. She reached into the drawer, pulled two bags of popcorn out and tossed one to Gabbie. Then asked O'Halleran, "How do you know that?"

"I just had a feeling after seeing her condo. The only thing in it was sexy lingerie, sex toys, and booze. Oh, and ten grand in the kitchen. That's why I went over to see my friend in vice and asked him if she was on their radar. It turns out that she was indeed on their to-do list. No pun intended. Got anymore popcorn? Because it gets better."

Jessica tossed him her unopened bag and said, "She had to be making bank selling real estate, why would she be turning tricks too?"

O'Halleran continued, "My source, who wishes to remain anonymous, said they thought she'd been at it for a long time. He had heard from an informant a few years back that it was a side hustle for her and she was very expensive. The funny thing is, vice planned to set up a sting operation but was told by the chief to leave her alone and find something else to do. Oh, and coincidentally the chief's car had been spotted outside her condo on numerous occasions.

Jessica shook her head, "One thing is for sure. There are no secrets on this island. I'm surprised she operated as long as she did without it being front page news. But if the chief was one of her clients that would explain a lot."

Jessica felt her cell phone vibrate in her pocket. She pulled it out, glanced down at it and saw it was Danica Bradshaw. "Speaking of front page news. I better take this."

"Hello, this is Jessica."

"Danica Bradshaw here, did you find the pendant?"

"No, we're still looking for it. Let me ask you a question. Do you have any idea why Bonnie wanted to meet you at the condo and not her office?"

"She said she was having her office fumigated and couldn't do the interview at home. She lives with her elderly mother who always sits in the living room watching TV with the volume up because she's hard of hearing and won't get hearing aids. It would be too disruptive to do the interview there and would be better to meet at her vacation rental that was vacant that day."

"Thanks. I got to go," Jessica said.

"Wait," Danica blurted before Jessica could hang up.

"I thought you would like to know there are rumors around town the serial killer might be a cop."

"Feel free to give me the name of a suspect next time you hear one mentioned in a rumor. But I might have something you would like to know. Hang on a second."

Jessica put Danica on hold and looked to O'Halleran. "Would you mind if I gave this reporter a taste of info about Bonnie James' secret side business?"

"Just a taste. Not the whole meal," he replied.

"This is off-the-record Danica. Bonnie James wasn't just a real estate broker as she appeared to be. Let's just say she had a side business working in the evenings with some of the most powerful people on this island."

"Are you saying she was a hooker?"

"That would be for you to find out."

Jessica hung up the phone and turned to her partners. "Now we have a next of kin to notify."

23

BONNIES' MOTHER

TUESDAY, MARCH 20TH.

After a quick check of the property tax records on the Kona side of the island, Jessica found two properties listed that belonged to Bonnie James. The first one listed was the condo where she was murdered. The one they didn't know about was a home in Keauhou Estates, where she lived.

The house was in a gated community overlooking an ocean front golf course with panoramic views of the coastline. Keauhou was about five and a half miles from the task force office. Gabbie drove her new 4Runner and Jessica was happy to let her as they took the scenic route along the coast.

When they arrived at the front gate of Keauhou Estates, Gabbie flashed her badge and the guard waved them through. They drove to the address listed and parked in front of the house.

There were three days' worth of newspapers laying in the driveway. But otherwise it looked like any other house on the street. Keauhou Estates used to be where all the rich people in Kona lived. Now it was an upper middle class neighborhood compared to the resort homes out on the coast north of Kailua.

Jessica and Gabbie walked up to the front door. The glass

side lights of the door had dolphins laser etched onto them. Looking through the clear parts of the glass, they could partially see through the house to the ocean. "Oh pretty," Gabbie said. Jessica nodded in agreement.

There was no answer after ringing the doorbell and knocking repeatedly. "Let's walk around to the backyard," Jessica said. Gabbie turned and started off on the left side of the house and Jessica went to the right. They met around back at the swimming pool. The sliding glass doors were open, and they could hear the TV blaring. The volume was up so high it would have been impossible to hear the doorbell inside the house.

"Hello, Police Department," Jessica yelled as she and Gabbie entered the home. To the right was the kitchen, and to the left was the living room. Bonnie's mother was sitting in a recliner in front of the TV, asleep. Jessica looked around to find the remote and saw that it was on a nearby coffee table. She grabbed it and turned off the TV. Bonnie's mother woke up when the room became silent.

The old woman asked, "Who are you," as her eyes focused on the strangers standing in her living room. "Detective Kealoha and Detective Gabbie Harris ma'am," Jessica answered.

"Why are you here?" The woman asked.

"We're looking for Zee Fleming, the mother of Bonnie James. Would that be you?"

"Yes," She answered.

"We have some terrible news to tell you. Someone strangled Bonnie two nights ago; she's dead."

Zee sighed after hearing the news but showed no emotion. She picked up the remote control for the chair she was sitting in and pressed a button on it that tilted the chair forward, helping her to stand up. As she stood up with the help of the chair she said, "Getting older isn't for sissies. Sitting's easy, getting up's a bitch when you're eighty-five."

The frail woman, with the help of Jessica and Gabbie, slowly walked across the room to a small desk that had a couple of drawers. She pulled the middle drawer open and took out a Gucci Planner and walked back over to the recliner and sat down with it. "This might help you find out who did it. And if not, it will definitely cause a lot of grief to some of the rat bastards that live on this island whose names are in it." The old woman held the planner out for Jessica to take.

Jessica and Gabbie both stared at what they didn't yet know was the equivalent of a little black book. "Thank you. Is there anyone we can call to come be with you?" Jessica asked Zee as Gabbie looked on.

"No, I have a son that lives on the mainland in Arizona. If I call him, he might want me to go live with him and I don't want to do that. I like it just fine here. It's too hot there."

Zee invited Jessica and Gabbie to sit and talk story for a while. They stayed for close to an hour.

"Most people would not approve of how Bonnie made her living. But she never asked any of them for a handout. So they can all go screw themselves. She paid her own way in life. And when a lot of people filed for bankruptcy, after the economy went in the toilet in 2009, she did what she had to do to pay the bills. I'm sad that it may have cost her her life. But I'm proud of what she accomplished. Look around. She earned it. Nothing was ever handed to her. Life was hard and then she died."

After Jessica and Gabbie left Bonnie's home, on the way back to the task force office, Jessica said, "Man, that was one hard core old woman," as she shook her head in disbelief.

"I'll second that," Gabbie added.

While Gabbie drove, Jessica opened the planner Zee had given them. It was twenty-eight pages that contained the names of celebrities and politicians from both the mainland and other islands in the state of Hawaii. A few minutes after reading a handful of pages she said to Gabbie, "This is better than one of those Desperate Housewives TV shows. The names of some powerful people with a dollar figure ranging from twelve hundred to nine grand next to each one of their names is in here." Jessica closed the book and said, "I can't wait to get back to office to read through it."

24

BLACK BOOK

MARCH 20TH, 4:45 P.M.

Jessica sat at her desk looking at page after page of Bonnie James' "little black book" which was really a red Gucci Planner. She recognized a lot of names, but none of them drew the shock that the one on the last page did–Sam Stewart.

She slammed the planner down on her desk hard enough that it bounced her coffee cup up so it spilled over the sides of the mug. There wasn't a dollar figure next to Sam's name, instead there were five stars. Jessica felt a sharp pang in her gut after her initial reaction of being madder than a hornet.

It didn't make any sense to her. She'd never suspected him of straying, and especially not with a hooker.

Below Sam's name were two other names rated at four stars and three stars, respectively. Both of them married and well-known multimillionaires on the island.

Jessica sat frozen while staring at the final page of Bonnie James' planner. She fixated on the last three names, wondering why they had stars next to them. She wondered if it was because Sam wasn't married that his name was at the top of the list.

Gabbie was sitting across from Jessica at her desk, filing

her nails while she held the phone up to her ear with her shoulder. She was listening to a citizen who was calling in a tip. She thanked the caller, said they'd be sure to check out his suspicious neighbor and hung up the phone. She was anxious to find out what Jessica was so upset about.

"Are you okay?" She asked.

Jessica slid the planner across her desk to Gabbie and said, "Turn to the last page."

Gabbie picked up the day-timer, opened it to the back page and started scanning from the top down. When she got near the bottom, and saw Sam's name, she stopped and looked up at Jessica, whose eyes were watering.

Jessica wasn't crying, but she was on the verge of it. "I'm going to the bathroom," she said.

"Okay," Gabbie said in a low tone of voice.

Jessica was an expert at sucking it up, because she'd had to her entire life. By the look on her face when she returned from the bathroom, it was as if the previous 10 minutes had never happened.

She asked Gabbie, "Any ideas about the stars behind Sam's name and the two others below him?"

Gabbie didn't hesitate, "She was looking for a husband, sugar daddy or someone to blackmail would be my guess."

Jessica said, "I didn't know what to think when I saw Sam's name. And to be honest, my first thought was that he had cheated. Which is irrational, because I don't have one shred of evidence other than his name being in that book."

"There is no way in hell that Sam cheated on you. I've seen the way he looks at you. Those are not the looks from a man who would stray. Trust me on that, Karl never looked at me like Sam looks at you."

Jessica slowly shook her head in agreement. She liked Gabbie's take on it, but she wanted to hear it straight from Sam, if he had any idea how his name got into Bonnie's planner.

It was near time to go home, and Jessica had enjoyed that day about all she could stand. In the old days it was Miller Time. Now it was bath time. That's all she wanted to do was go home, take a hot bubble bath and try not to think about anything for maybe twenty or thirty minutes.

Before Jessica went home for the night, she took off her badge and handed it to Gabbie. "We both know, as soon as O'Halleran finds out Sam's name is in Bonnie's little black book, I'm as good as off the case. I have no interest in riding a desk at the Kona station or working cases unrelated to the serial killer. Finding the killer was the only reason I signed on for this. You're probably thinking "what the hell" right about now. I don't blame you. I'm sorry. We'll talk tomorrow. I got to go home and think about all of this."

"Oh, hell no. You're going to tell him yourself," Gabbie said, as she slid the badge back across her desk toward Jessica.

Jessica reluctantly picked it up before leaving.

It was close to sunset as she drove home along the coast on Alii Drive, and the sky was a bright red orange that evening. The waves were small and there were only a couple of vehicles parked across from Lyman's Bay as she passed by. One vehicle was an old rusty lifted Toyota truck that belonged to a pot dealer who had always sold weed there. The other vehicle was most likely a customer since they had parked side by side off in the corner of the parking lot.

Some things never change, she thought, as she passed by the place where people had sold weed for as long as she could remember.

She tried her best to get her head in the right place before she got home. She didn't want to come off accusatory when she asked Sam about Bonnie James, although she felt she had every right to give him the third degree. What really sounded good was stopping off at the bar next to Magic Sands and having a drink. But she knew that was no longer a choice in her life and was glad she felt a relief when she cruised by the bar and had no sudden urge to stop in and knock one back.

Less than ten minutes later she was home and clicking the button on the garage door opener above her visor to open the door. Sam was already home. He had picked up Henry from daycare and already had him in the bathtub, to decontaminate from the virus of the week while Sam went to the kitchen to get something to drink.

"Hi honey, how was your day?" Sam asked as Jessica walked into the house from the garage. He was pouring a glass of iced tea.

She couldn't help herself and glared at him for a moment before she answered, "It sucked."

"What?"

"Earlier today, Gabbie and I took possession of the equivalent of a little black book from a dead hooker's mother. The book contained thirty pages of who's who on the island. Like celebrities, politicians and miscellaneous rich guys. And guess whose name was in miscellaneous rich guy section? Don't answer, I'll tell you–yours."

Sam stood there looking dumbfounded. "How?"

Jessica struggled to stay calm as she set her purse on the kitchen counter and said, "I was hoping you could tell me that." She pulled her Glock out of its holster and said, "I'm going to put this in the gun safe so no one accidentally gets shot and then I'm going to go take a bath. After Henry goes to bed, we should talk."

***

They were sitting in the living room after putting Henry to bed.

"Have you ever met with Bonnie James? Did she ever give you a thorough tour of the bedroom?" Jessica asked in a serious tone of voice.

Sam looked at her, puzzled. The questions surprised him. It was suddenly starting to sound like an interrogation.

With a tone of annoyance in his voice, Sam said, "I'm not sure what you're getting at here, but you're barking up the wrong tree. I barely knew her. I met her once to go look at a couple of lots for sale up behind Costco. I was interested in the property so I could build a warehouse to store a surplus of boat building supplies for the yacht business. Then after that I had Pua handle all communication with her."

Jessica continued to glare at Sam. Unlike when she was interviewing a suspect, where she had no emotional skin in the game, this was different, and it showed when her tone became accusatory as she questioned Sam. "Why the hell was your name in her book and she had five stars behind your name? There were two other men listed underneath your name, both very wealthy, too. They had stars behind their names as well. Everybody else in that book had a dollar figure next to their name. What was the deal? Were you her sugar daddy?"

Sam got up from the couch and said, "You're insane. I'm going to work out." He left the room and went to the gym at the far end of the house. Jessica went out on the lanai and sat down in a chair overlooking the bay. She listened to the surf and took in a deep breath of the salt air because it always calmed her. She had lost control in there and she knew it.

She'd interrogated thousands of suspects over her career, and she could tell most of the time when somebody was lying. She didn't think Sam was lying after she had pushed him past the point of making him mad, which she then regretted, but she still wasn't a hundred percent sure if he was innocent.

25

JESSICA CAN'T SLEEP

The bags under Jessica's eyes were getting big enough to pack for vacation. The latest revelation of Sam's name in the back of Bonnie James' little black book wasn't helping her sleep either.

It was one thirty in the morning when she woke up. She got out of bed and went to the kitchen and grabbed a notepad and pen that were sitting on the counter next to the phone. She was skeptical about whether Dr. Williams' plan of writing about her demons would help.

But since she was still not sleeping, she figured she had nothing to lose. If she was going to be awake, she might as well make the best of it.

She sat at the kitchen table holding the pen and stared at the blank notepad for close to seven minutes before she put one word down. The first word she wrote was Sam. She stared at the paper for another minute before adding another word, and then it was thirty seconds until the next one. One word after the next followed and soon she had a paragraph.

About every other word she had written had a four letter word starting with "F". Eventually, she muttered, "F this, I'm going to bed." She tore the page off of the notepad, crumpled it up and threw it in the trash can underneath the sink.

After she returned to bed, she lay her head on the pillow and exhaled a sigh of momentary relief. She had no idea what had just happened in the kitchen, but, for a second she felt like maybe that quack she'd been going to see might be on to something.

The one thing she was sure of was that anything she wrote was going to go in the trash immediately thereafter, so it could never be used against her by anyone in court or out.

She knew she had a lot of skeletons in the closet that needed to be pulled out and dusted off. And maybe even get rid of a few of them. But she had to be careful because there was one skeleton that was going to stay in the closet no matter what. She had vowed to never discuss it ever again with Gabbie or anyone else.

***

Jessica was in the kitchen making coffee when the doorbell rang. It was Auntie May; she was there to pick up Henry. "Mahalo Auntie for taking Henry today for us," Jessica said.

"No worries, it's on the way." Jessica hugged Henry and kissed him on the cheek. She walked out the front door with them, stopping short at the grass. She watched Henry following Auntie May toward the old Toyota Tercel parked in front of the house.

While Jessica was waving at Henry and Auntie May as they drove away, Sam had come into the kitchen and poured himself a cup of coffee. He was sitting at the dining room table when she came back into the kitchen. He didn't look much happier than he did the night before, when he went to work out, after walking away from Jessica's interrogation.

They hadn't talked since then because he had gone into his study after working out and stayed there until midnight. He went to bed after Jessica and had gotten up early, to take his kayak out, before she got up.

Sam didn't say anything as he stirred his coffee with a spoon. Jessica could tell he was still upset. He didn't put cream or sugar in his coffee, but he always stirred it when he was angry.

"I'm sorry. I shouldn't have come at you like that," Jessica said. Sam nodded as he got up from the table and started toward the garage. "I have to go to work," he said as he walked by Jessica without stopping to kiss her goodbye.

It was clear he was still mad, he had never done that. But then they'd never had the type of conversation that they had the night before.

After Sam had left for work, Jessica took her cup of coffee out to the lanai and stared mindlessly at the turquoise blue bay, while sipping her coffee. She let her mind wander and tried not to focus on any thought. She was sorry about giving Sam the third degree. But she wasn't sure he was innocent, until he had left the house that morning.

She realized she would need to put as much effort into making it right as she put into making it wrong, and promised herself she would do so that evening.

26

CONFLICT OF INTEREST

As Jessica drove to the task force office, her mind raced as she thought about the possible implications of Sam's name in the dead hooker's little black book.

She knew there was a good chance that every name in the book would become public, and the last thing she wanted was to see Sam's name dragged through the mud. By the time she got to the office, she had changed her mind a couple of times as to what she should do.

The last thing she wanted to do was tamper with evidence. But she also did not want to see Sam's reputation tarnished. The five stars behind his name in some hooker's ledger didn't prove anything. But if it became known that his name was in Bonnie's book, it would be devastating to his reputation worldwide and he didn't deserve that. He was her man, and she wanted to protect him by removing the page with his name in Bonnie's day-timer. But she couldn't jeopardize the case–ultimately it was more important.

After she arrived at the office, the first thing she did was grab Bonnie's planner off of Gabbie's desk. She opened it and found that the last page, with Sam's name on it, was missing.

Minutes later as she stared at the planner, she could hear Gabbie and O'Halleran climbing up the stairs. She quickly slid the book back over to Gabbie's desk before they walked in. Jessica got up, opened the door and held it for them. Gabbie was carrying a box of donuts and O'Halleran had the coffee.

After O'Halleran set the coffees down, he went back to his car to get his blood pressure medicine that he'd forgotten. While he was downstairs at his car Jessica asked Gabbie, "What happened to the last page?"

Gabbie picked up Bonnie's planner and opened it. She looked at it for a moment then said, "I don't see a problem here. The page you're looking for is irrelevant. If you want to put it back, you can–after we catch the killer. But if you think you're leaving me here to work with O'Halleran, that's not happening. I only took this job because you asked me to help you. And now you want to fall on your sword?"

Before Jessica could reply, she heard O'Halleran's footsteps coming up the stairs and didn't answer Gabbie. O'Halleran couldn't find the medication he was looking for and said that he had to go home and get it. He said he'd be back in a while.

After O'Halleran pulled out of the driveway, Jessica said, "The last page has to go back in. I appreciate what you did. But this investigation has to be by the book. When we find the killer I don't want it coming out in court, somehow, that we tampered with the evidence."

Gabbie sat at her desk and took a bite of her malasada. She chewed it slowly while she gave Jessica some serious stink-eye. After she swallowed the last bite, and licked the cream off her fingers, she said, "I'm going to quit when they take you off the case."

Jessica nodded. "I get it. I know you only took the job because I asked you to. I'm sorry I've put you in this situation." Jessica picked up her glazed donut, took a bite and quickly swallowed it. "What if we continued the investigation on our own?" she said.

Gabbie took a sip of her coffee and set the cup down. She opened the bottom right drawer of her desk and reached down into the bottom. After rifling underneath a stack of papers, she pulled out the missing last page.

"I'm still mad at you. But we'll work it out. Let's get the DNA information before we do anything else," Gabbie said.

Jessica nodded and began cleaning out her desk. She knew what was coming as soon as O'Halleran returned and found out Sam's name was in their victim's book.

Gabbie checked her email and saw the DNA results from under Bonnie's fingernails had come back.

"The crime lab didn't get a hit in the DNA database," she said.

Jessica looked up and said, "Ask your friend at the lab if they can at least tell us the region the DNA is from. I want to know if it's from Europe, Germany in particular; see if they can narrow it down that much."

"Okay, I'm on it." Gabbie picked up her phone and called the lab. Ten minutes later, she got off the phone with her contact. "He says the DNA sample was from a male and had German ancestry. He also said the DNA on the fingernails matched the DNA we found on the money."

Jessica slowly sat back in her chair behind the desk and looked at Gabbie. "We need to call the German feds and ask them to search their records of Dieter and Hans Schilling and find out if they had another brother. Also, what their father's name was and how old and where he or they are right now."

"You think this might have something to do with the serial killers on the island years ago?" Gabbie asked.

"We'll see where the evidence leads us. But I got a bad feeling about this."

Jessica checked what time it was in Berlin and saw it was about three o'clock in the morning. "I'll call the German police tonight when they're starting their day and see if they can help us.

***

O'Halleran walked into the office holding a prescription bottle. Little did he know how much he was going to need that blood pressure medication that he'd gone home for.

Jessica had already packed up her desk and put it in a box. When O'Halleran showed up he saw the box sitting on top of her desk. With a confused look on his face, he asked, "What's going on?"

Jessica was holding Bonnie's day-timer while she leaned against her desk. "We have a problem. Actually, I have a problem," Jessica said, as she handed the book to O'Halleran.

"What's this?" he asked.

"It's Bonnie James' little black book."

"And how is this a problem?" he asked while still looking somewhat confused.

"My fiancé, Sam Stewart's name is in it."

O'Halleran opened the book and briefly thumbed through the pages, looking at the names and the dollar figures next to them.

"Turn to the back page and you'll see it."

He turned to the page and studied it about ten seconds. "No dollar figure, just stars next to his name. It's not up to me. But if it was, this wouldn't be a problem. But I'm going to have to run it up the chain of command and we'll see what they have to say. But you're still on the job until I hear otherwise."

O'Halleran went to his desk and called the District Attorney. After a lengthy conversation he said, "King will get back to me in the morning. But it doesn't sound good."

27

SAM

Before Jessica left work, she called Sam and told him she was picking up dinner. She wanted to meet at Kahaluu Beach Park to eat and watch the sunset together. He didn't sound too thrilled to hear her voice, but said he and Henry would meet her there in thirty minutes, at the small pavilion.

She stopped at L&L Barbecue and got two mixed plates for dinner. She ordered Sam his favorite, which was barbecue chicken with potato mac salad. For her and Henry it was going to be chicken katsu with white rice and soy sauce.

When she pulled into the parking lot, she looked over toward the small pavilion and saw Sam and Henry sitting there waiting. They sat on top of the picnic table with their backs to her, watching the surfers and people snorkeling in the bay. It was about 6:30 p.m., and less than a half hour from sundown. It was a perfect late afternoon to have a picnic while watching the sunset.

As Jessica approached the pavilion, Sam caught a glimpse of her out of the corner of his eye but ignored her until she got to the table. She sat the bag with food down on top of it and started pulling out the mixed plate dinners. "Hi, honey," she said, as she leaned over to kiss Sam. He replied with a soft

"Hi." Henry was hungry and skipped the greeting formalities and went straight to an enthusiastic, "What are we having for dinner?"

"You and I are having chicken katsu," Jessica answered. Henry smiled; he liked chicken katsu because it was almost like chicken McNuggets, which was his favorite. The three of them sat there eating while they watched the sun drop toward the horizon, as surfers caught the last waves of the day before dusk. After they finished eating, Jessica suggested they go sit on the beach for a bit, which was fine with Henry because he had wanted to go over there since they had arrived and Sam had kept telling him no.

"Go ahead and play right over there," Jessica pointed to a close by area on the small beach between the pavilion and St. Peters Church at the opposite end. She and Sam would be able to keep an eye on him and have a private conversation at the same time.

They sat in the sand next to the lifeguard tower and after Henry was out of earshot, Jessica turned toward Sam and said, "I'm sorry about the way I questioned you last night. I should have trusted you."

Sam continued to look straight ahead as the sun got closer to the horizon and said, "Yes, you should have."

"My ex cheated on me and I swore I'd never be so blind the next time. I know that doesn't make it better, but I hope it helps explain why I overreacted. I did some writing last night about it. I've been stuffing a lot of crap over the years and I haven't done a very good job of taking care of myself mentally."

Sam reached his arm around her shoulder and pulled her closer to him.

"I probably overreacted a little bit myself. I'm sorry, too."

"It won't happen again. Unless of course I think you're guilty as sin," she said with a straight face and then giggled.

Sam turned his head that time, leaned over and kissed her

on the lips softly, just in time to hear Henry say "Yuck," as he trotted across the beach, back to where they were sitting.

Henry wriggled his body down between Sam and Jessica. The three of them watched the sun rest on the horizon like a big orange ball. It remained there for what seemed like forever before it disappeared.

A few minutes after the sun was out of sight and it grew darker, they went home. Later that evening after Henry had bathed and gone to bed, Sam and Jessica sat in the living room on the couch facing Keauhou Bay. They watched a tour boat pass by the living room windows, as it came into dock, after its evening dinner cruise.

"I liked our dinner better," Sam said as Jessica snuggled in under his arm and leaned her head on his shoulder. "Me too," she said. They sat there and watched the tourists disembarking for a few minutes, while just enjoying the moment, before Jessica broke the silence.

"I'm probably going to get kicked off the task force."

"Because of my name being in that book?" Sam asked.

She nodded.

"Now I see another reason why you were so mad last night. You must have known then?"

"Yes, but it still wasn't right on my part to take it out on you."

Sam nodded and hugged her tightly. "What are you going to do now?" he said.

"Even though I'm not going to be on the task force any longer, probably after tomorrow, Gabbie and I will continue working together. We have to."

"Can't you just let it go and let her and O'Halleran handle it?"

"Not this time. I don't have the evidence yet, but if my suspicions are right, this case may tie into when my girlfriend Malia was murdered years ago. There may have been an unknown third killer at the time who has come back to the island. And if that's true, it means I'm not safe from being a target." Jessica glanced at the clock on the wall and saw it was just after 9:30 p.m.

"I have to call the German Federal Police now since it's about 9:00 a.m. there." She got up from the couch, kissed Sam and went into the study to make the call.

28

SOLVED LANCASTER

The next morning O'Halleran went to Hilo to have a face-to-face meeting with the district attorney and the chief of police. That afternoon when he returned to the task force office, he had a deal for Jessica. The two women were sitting at their desks when he walked in the office. "You will be off the Bonnie James case. But you can work on all the other cases that are in the scope of the investigation of the serial killer."

Jessica nodded and said, "I guess I'll go get my office box out of the trunk of my car. Speaking of other cases, Gabbie and I've been looking at the Lancaster murder and we don't think our serial killer did it. The medical examiner's report came back and it said that whoever strangled him used a wide strap, most likely a belt. Our guy uses a garrote that isn't much thicker than a shoelace."

Earlier that day Jessica had done some digging and found out that Mr. Lancaster had a million dollar life insurance policy. His wife was the benefactor in the event of his demise. After she got off the phone with the insurance company, Jessica said to Gabbie, "We have a motive. Let's take a drive out to Kukio, take a look at their security video and then go chat with Mrs. Lancaster."

The Kukio resort security supervisor was happy to let Jessica and Gabbie review the footage on the street where the Lancaster's home was. It didn't take him long to find a clip that showed the neighbor, Jerry Scott from across the street, walk over to the Lancaster residence on the afternoon of the murder. Then five minutes later leave and walk back to his house. It showed him wearing Levi's and a belt when he went over. But he was carrying the belt when he walked back home. Jessica asked the security supervisor, "Do you know his name?"

"Yeah, that's Jerry Scott. He's a trust fund baby. He's a real dirtbag. He's been here maybe six or seven months. He doesn't own the house, he lives with his aunt. He is single-handedly responsible for ninety-nine percent of the noise complaints here at the resort. Whenever we get a call from an irate homeowner about somebody racing a motorcycle up and down the street, it's that guy. He's bad news. We always send Kaleo to go talk to him."

"Why Kaleo?" Jessica asked.

"He fights MMA besides working security here, and Jerry Scott doesn't give him any grief. The rest of us, he threatens. But not Kaleo," the guard said.

"Can we borrow Kaleo?" Gabbie joked. Jessica cut her eyes to Gabbie. "Just kidding," she said.

After watching the security videos, Jessica and Gabbie left the security office and ran Jerry Scott's name–he was on parole for attempted murder. They drove to his house across from the Lancaster's. When they knocked on the door Scott opened it, then tried to slam it shut. Jessica had her collapsible baton in hand and stuck it between the door and the jamb, preventing the door from closing. The door slammed into the baton, bounced back and hit Scott in the face, momentarily stunning him.

Jessica and Gabbie pushed the door open and had him on the ground in handcuffs after a brief struggle. Eva Lancaster was naked in the living room screaming, "Let him go. He didn't do anything! You're going to be sorry–I'm calling my dad, he's a lawyer."

Jessica and Gabbie walked Scott out to the car and put him in the backseat. Gabbie stayed with him, while Jessica went back in to talk to Mrs. Lancaster. Apparently her dad really was a lawyer. And the first thing he had told his daughter to do was ask Jessica if she was under arrest. If not, tell the police she won't be answering any questions, they can call her father from now on. By that time, the newly widowed wife had gotten dressed and pulled her father's business card out of her purse to give to Jessica.

Jessica walked out to the car and tossed the business card to Gabbie as she got in. "She lawyered up."

On the other hand, twenty minutes later on the ride back to Kona, their suspect had not. After Jessica told Scott, Eva had taken out a million dollar life insurance policy, he was more than happy to roll over on her. "A million? That bitch! It was all her idea," he said. "She told me I would get fifty grand for offing him when she collected the insurance money. She said I had to strangle him to make it look like the Kona Strangler had done it. She said it would work, since her husband was a real estate developer–the strangler was only offing real estate people."

They took Scott to the Kona cellblock and booked him for first degree murder after they had a written confession from him. Afterward, Gabbie quipped, "What a funny world when you believe the murderer more than you do the non-murderer."

The next stop was the on-call judge's home to get a warrant signed for Eva Lancaster's arrest. After Jessica got his signature on the warrant, she and Gabbie were on a mission. "One down, one to go," Gabbie said.

Jessica nodded and said, "Let's go arrest that bitch."

After driving back to the Kukio Resort, it was almost 9 p.m. when Jessica and Gabbie pounded on the front door of the Lancaster residence. Eva Lancaster opened the door and, just like her partner in crime, she attempted to slam it in Jessica's face. And just like Scott, it ended with her in handcuffs, face down on the ground.

"I want to call my dad," she screamed as they were putting her into the back of the car.

Jessica answered, "Right after we book you for murder."

29

GERMAN POLICE

The next morning when Jessica and Gabbie got to the office, O'Halleran was there waiting for them with a box of donuts. "You guys kicked some serious ass yesterday on the Lancaster case. Have a donut," he said as he held out the box with the lid open.

"One down, one to go," Jessica said and Gabbie nodded.

O'Halleran looked at Jessica. "You're on the Gorky case now and Gabbie and I'll work on Bonnie James." The smile on her face evaporated, but she knew that was the way it was going to be. And she decided that it was better than being kicked off the task force altogether which is what she thought was going to happen.

Before work that morning she had told Sam, over their morning coffee out on the lanai, that the brass had removed her from working the Bonnie James case, but not the task force. And that was a reasonable compromise she could live with.

Jessica sat down at her desk and checked her email while she ate a glazed donut. At once she saw she'd gotten a response from the German police. The Germans said Dieter Schilling had a twin brother, named Ulrich, who had been in a

German prison two years after Dieter murdered Malia twenty-four years earlier. Ulrich had served 20 years for a murder he'd committed in Berlin. They released him three years ago, according to their records.

Jessica set the rest of her donut down on her desk and slid back into her chair. She spun it around to look out the window at the ocean while she thought about the email she had just read.

After a few minutes of contemplation, she slowly turned back to her desk and asked Gabbie, "Come check this out and bring the murder book."

After Gabbie came around to Jessica's desk with the murder book, Jessica opened it. They both looked at the photo of the crowd of bystanders on the beach, that she had taken at Hapuna where Pam Gorky was found dead. They both studied Ulrich Schilling's mug shot, in the email from the German Police that was still open on the desktop in front of them.

"Jessica looked up at Gabbie, who had been looking over her shoulder and asked, "Do you see him in that beach photo?" Gabbie shook her head no. "Me neither, but the ones wearing hats and sunglasses make it impossible to know for sure."

Gabbie and O'Halleran left the office to go talk to Bonnie James' mother, Zee. They needed to ask her if she had any knowledge about the men listed in Bonnie's day-timer, aka "the little black book," and particularly if she knew why there were stars next to Sam's name and the others.

While they were out of the office, Jessica started looking at Hawaii driver's license records to see if anyone with the name of Ulrich Adolph Schilling had applied for one. She wondered if he had come to Hawaii like his brothers had years earlier. After a quick database search, his name popped up. It was just shy of three years ago that the state had issued a driver's license to one Ulrich Adolph Schilling in Kona.

Reading that made the hair on her arm stand up. But when she looked at his photo, it looked nothing like the photo the German police had sent her.

She shot off a quick email asking them if there might have been a mix-up in the photo they had sent. It was the middle of the night in Berlin, so she'd have to wait until the next day before she would get a response back from them.

Jessica decided to check the Hawaii state occupational license website to see if there were any business or professional licenses registered to an Ulrich Schilling. After five minutes of searching, she sat there staring at her computer screen dumbfounded. She had found him. He was listed as the CEO of D&H Realty in Kona. She could feel her heart racing and her head getting light. This was Dieter and Hans' brother. Now the question in her mind was if he was a serial killer too, just like his brothers.

The next step would be to try to get a DNA sample from him. She jotted down his office location on a notepad, ripped the top sheet off and stuck it in her shirt pocket. The address was to a large office in the old industrial area. She knew exactly where it was.

It was located in an older strip mall near the highway. She jumped in her car and drove to D&H Realty to get a look at it. It became apparent that she wasn't going to be able to dig through the trash and find something with Ulrich's DNA on it, since the real estate office used a community dumpster.

Jessica drove back to the task force office. Her adrenaline was pumping the whole time, so much so she could barely keep her foot on the gas pedal. The feeling was intoxicating; she had missed it, and it was good to feel it again. Now she had to figure out a way to get Ulrich Schilling's DNA.

***

When Jessica got back to the office, Gabbie and O'Halleran were there. When she walked in the door she looked like she was floating three inches off the floor. It was obvious by the look on her face that something was up. Gabbie was the first ask, "You look like the Cheshire cat. Did you go home for a nooner or something?" Jessica smiled, "I hadn't thought of that, but I might now. But first I need to tell you what I found out."

After she showed Gabbie and O'Halleran all the evidence that she had found earlier, she asked them, "Any suggestions how we're going to get his DNA?"

O'Halleran said, "He's German, Germans drink beer at Oktoberfest, or in this case the Kona Brew Fest. That's coming up at the end of the month. No self-respecting German on the island would miss it."

"We need to make sure he shows up there so we can snatch up his cup after he throws it in the trash," Jessica said.

"How are we going to do that?" asked Gabbie.

"Maybe we can get him to think he's going to meet a high-end client. If I know one thing about a lot of real estate people, it's they all want to be rich. We just need to lead him to the trough," Jessica said.

"That's an excellent idea," O'Halleran concurred and Gabbie nodded.

That night, when Jessica went home, she said to Sam, "Honey, I need a favor."

"Sure, what do you need?"

"I need you to go to the Brew Fest on Saturday. You'll act like you want to buy something expensive enough to entice a certain real estate broker to meet with you there for a couple beers."

"This isn't going to turn out to be something like the time I got shot in the leg is it?"

"No, he won't use a gun. He's more of the type that likes to use a garrote to strangle people. And since there will be hundreds of people there, I doubt he'll try to do it in public," she joked.

"Oh, I can't wait," Sam said with obvious sarcasm.

30

DANICA GETS A LETTER

Danica Bradshaw got another letter in the mail addressed to her at the newspaper. It read, *"I don't have any manifestos I feel need posted in your newspaper. But I have a couple of comments to make. Your post of the manifesto you published was the work of a plagiarist who was delusional. Of course, I had to punish him for trying to take credit for my work. Wrapped inside the envelope is something that will prove that I am the real deal; unlike the imposter who sent you the diatribe you printed. You're lucky I've decided to spare you."*

Danica stopped reading the letter and looked back inside the large vanilla envelope. At the bottom was something wrapped in paper and tape. She had missed it when she pulled the letter from the envelope. She pulled it out, grabbed the scissors off her desk and delicately cut the tape so she could unwrap what was a piece of jewelry. It was the diamond pendant awarded to Bonnie James at the real estate awards ceremony.

Danica was careful about how she picked it up, trying not to get her fingerprints on it. She carefully set it on her desk, grabbed her phone and dialed Jessica. When she answered,

Danica blurted out, "I've gotten something in the mail you will want to see."

"Please tell me it's not another manifesto from a whack job," Jessica replied.

"Oh no, it's way better than that. It's Bonnie James' ruby and diamond pendant."

"Please don't touch it anymore. I'm on my way."

Danica hung up the phone and picked the letter back up to finish reading it. She had almost forgotten she hadn't finished reading it in her frenzy to call Jessica. She continued to read the letter from where she had left off. The next paragraph said, *"The second point I wish to make is: twenty-four years ago there were three of us who hunted women. Not two, as reported in your paper. We had taken a souvenir from one victim that was never publicized in news reports. If you check, you'll find there was never a mention of an amputated foot, found in our treasure trove we took from the victims. What can I say, one of us had a foot fetish."*

Danica was sitting at her desk, guarding the piece of jewelry as if her life depended on it, still stunned from the letter, when Jessica and Gabbie walked into the newsroom.

"I was super careful about how I picked it up and tried not to get my fingerprints on it. He says in the letter that there were three killers hunting women on the island years ago. He mentioned they had amputated a foot from one victim and said the Herald had never disclosed it in news reports. He's right; I looked it up. There was never any disclosure about it in the paper," Danica said.

Jessica and Gabbie took possession of the pendant and the letter from Danica and thanked her. Gabbie took the pendant to the Kona police station to have it dusted for fingerprints. And Jessica went back to see Sid Akiona to ask him about the foot.

***

Sid was sitting on the lanai smoking a joint when Jessica

pulled into the driveway. She was downwind and could smell it as soon as she got out of the car.

"I love retirement. I just sit out here and get stoned when I feel like it. I don't give a crap about who does what or why anymore," Sid said as Jessica walked up to the lanai.

"You know that stuff will make you stupid, right?" Jessica said.

"That's probably true for chronic users. But I only smoke it once in a while for pain relief. The doctors wanted to put me on pain pills and I said no way."

"Your back's still bothering you?"

"Yeah. Well, not now," Sid smiled as he looked at what was left of the joint he had put out.

"The reason I'm here, Sid, is that something came up today that I need to ask you about. I just came from The Herald. One of their reporters got a letter in the mail today, allegedly from the serial killer. He wrote that there were three killers operating when Malia was murdered years ago."

That got Sid's attention. He straightened up in his chair and said, "No shit? It's just like I told you before. I always thought there were three. But how do we know he's telling the truth?"

"That's why I'm here. I was hoping you could help me with that. He said there was an amputated foot from one of the victims that was never mentioned in the press. Do you know if that was true?"

Sid was half-baked, but the look on his face grew serious, he nodded and said, "That's true, we never released that information to the public."

That revelation shook Jessica to her core. For twenty-four years she had thought there were only two serial killers working together. Now she knew, beyond any doubt, that there were three.

"Thanks, I appreciate your help, Sid. I have to run, I have an appointment. But I'll keep you in the loop."

Sid nodded and picked up his joint and relit it as Jessica walked back to her car.

Jessica's next appointment was with Dr. Williams. She really wanted to skip it but thought better of it since his previous advice had helped her get some sleep for a change.

31

DR. WILLIAMS

It was raining when Jessica arrived a few minutes early for her now weekly session with Dr. Williams. The dark clouds hovering over the island mirrored how she felt after learning earlier that there was a third serial killer. She sat in the waiting room thinking she couldn't wait for the Brew Fest at the end of the month. She had to try to get Ulrich Shilling's DNA sooner than later.

Dr. Williams opened the door, interrupting her train of thought, and invited her into his office. She sat at the same spot on the couch where she had sat the week before. This time when she looked out his window toward the ocean, the sky was dark and it was raining so hard the drops looked like they were bouncing off the surface of the ocean.

Dr. Williams reviewed his notes from their previous session, then he paused and took a good look at Jessica's face. "You look better. It looks like you've been getting some sleep."

She nodded and said, "It seems like the writing you asked me to do is helping–who would have thought."

He smiled. "Good. Why do you think that is?"

"I'm not getting the nightmares every night now."

Dr. Williams nodded. "Keep writing. It's taking the power out of the things that have been bothering you. It's not a total fix, but it's a start in the right direction. It's kinda like peeling an onion one ring at a time. This will take a while, but eventually, if you do the work, the nightmares should go away for good."

Jessica looked at him with skepticism, but had to admit his first suggestion was helping, so she might as well keep doing what he recommended. They spent the next hour going over the highlights of most of the things she had written about. It was mainly about her guilt concerning friends who had died and how she had been powerless to help them before it was too late. For years she had drowned those feelings of guilt with alcohol. But now she had to work through them once and for all, for her sake, and the sake of her family.

She told him about the guilt she carried about Henry's mother, Aimee. "If she hadn't been in my Jeep, she would still be alive today," Jessica said as she reached for the tissue box on the table next to the couch. She took one out and dabbed her eyes.

The murder of the week didn't bother her. But feeling like she was responsible for Aimee's death troubled her every day.

"I want you to take home this workbook and do the exercises in it. It will help with your PTSD." Dr. Williams handed it to Jessica just before she left his office. It was real growth for her. Before, she would have said "no thanks," but now she was at least willing to try, which was a huge step in the right direction.

She felt conflicted when she left Dr. Williams' office. She didn't want to spend any more time working on herself, when she could be working on getting Ulrich Schilling's DNA, which was now job one for her.

32

RAIN

Jessica had forgotten her umbrella that morning, and she got soaked by the time she crossed the parking lot from her car to the task force office. At least it was a warm rain, she thought, as she hurried to get under the cover of the building's eave. When she walked in the office, Gabbie and O'Halleran were on their phones.

The first thing she did was check her email. The German police had replied to the email she had sent them the previous day. They had found they had sent the wrong photo to her in their first response. This time they had attached the correct photo, and it looked just like Ulrich's Hawaii driver's license photo. Now she knew for sure that the Ulrich Schilling in Kona was the same one from Germany, and a brother of Dieter and Hans. Now getting his DNA was the most important next step to see if he was their current serial killer.

Ulrich looked nothing like Dieter or Hans from what she recalled; it had been a long time since she had seen the other Schilling brothers. Ulrich had aged considerably over the years, most likely from the stress of twenty years in prison.

Jessica went to the makeshift kitchen in the small office and got a cup of coffee. She took a sip and noted, if she wanted to drink coffee that didn't taste like expresso, she was going to have to make it herself. She set the cup down and put some cream in the brew to mellow it out.

Once Gabbie had gotten off the phone, she went into the kitchen for more coffee. As she was pouring herself a cup, Jessica asked, "Did you make that?" Gabbie shook her head no.

"That's right, you put a ton of sugar and cream in yours, so you would hardly notice a difference." Jessica took another sip and decided it was tolerable as long as it had enough cream. After she took another sip, she asked Gabbie, "What did Zee have to say yesterday?"

While Gabbie added more cream and sugar to her coffee she answered, "You're going to like this. It turns out O'Halleran knew her from Honolulu. She wasn't quite the innocent little old lady that we thought she was. He said she was a madam in the red-light district of Chinatown for over twenty years."

"You're kidding me?"

Gabbie shook her head no.

"Do you think she might still be running a string of girls?"

"O'Halleran pressed her hard, and she swore she was out of the business now. But she said one thing that was interesting. She had urged Bonnie to make a list of the ultra-wealthy men on the island that she could entice into a steady relationship. Then she could give up the half-dozen tourists she was doing each week."

Jessica had been stirring her coffee between sips the entire time, but stopped when Gabbie mentioned the list of ultra-wealthy men.

Gabbie continued, "The stars by Sam's and the other names meant they were prospects that Zee had picked as being good targets. She said she had recommended them to Bonnie after seeing their names over and over in the news and having checked out their net worths."

It was a bittersweet moment for Jessica. Now there was concrete proof Sam had never cheated. But it pissed her off that Bonnie had targeted him.

O'Halleran had finished his phone call and came over to get coffee, too. He said to Jessica, "You're back on the Bonnie James case. I just got it cleared with the chief of police and with the blessing of the D.A.

"I just told her about how Sam's name got in Bonnie's little black book," Gabbie said. "Great," O'Halleran said, as he poured a cup of coffee.

Jessica smiled for the first time at work that week and said, "Things are coming together. I got a response from the Germans this morning, and the original photo they sent was wrong. The new photo they included matches up with Ulrich Schilling's driver's license photo."

"Excellent work detective," O'Halleran said. The three of them returned to their desks and continued following up leads that morning before breaking for lunch. The usual routine was O'Halleran went down to The Office tavern for his daily liquid lunch. Jessica and Gabbie usually went to Lava Java across from Kailua Bay and had salads. Lava Java was open-air, had delicious food and a fantastic view of Kailua Bay. It was a great place to go, to take a break from the tension, in the middle of the day.

Jessica and Gabbie were regulars there and all the staff knew what they always ordered; two iced teas and a Cobb salad, with an extra plate so they could share.

The sky had cleared from the early morning showers, as was typical in Kona. If someone had just gotten out of bed and gone outside, they wouldn't have known it had rained earlier that day.

They had a solid suspect. Sam wasn't a cheater, and the air was clean. Things were looking up in Jessica's world view.

33

PUA

Ulrich thought about how he was going to take her out. He knew Dieter had used a spear gun to do his last murder because he had read about it while he was in prison. That technique seemed so distasteful; he preferred strangling his victims. It was quiet, it got the job done, and it didn't make a mess. He preferred to think of himself as more refined compared to his brothers when it came to the art of killing.

He had been watching Pua for a week. She had closed a lot of seven-figure real estate transactions in the last six months that should have been his. That was his goal. Sell more real estate on the island than anyone else and kill all of his top competitors. His brothers, Dieter and Hans, liked to kill for sport. For Ulrich, it was all about the money.

The only thing consistent about Pua was she went for a run on Alii Drive four days a week at 6:30 a.m. Three days a week she'd go to the Kona pier; she always swam to the fourth buoy. She would do four laps out and back, then go home to get ready for work.

He decided that taking her out so close to the pier was too risky and aborted the idea. Instead, he would kill her at an open house she was hosting later in the day.

Ulrich waited down the street from the open house and watched people come and go before making his move. When he was sure the house was empty, except for Pua, he walked in, looking around as if he was an interested buyer.

Pua greeted him and said, "Feel free to look around." He nodded but didn't say anything. She didn't recognize him because he was wearing a wig and sunglasses.

He looked around the living room and kitchen for a couple of minutes before heading to the back of the house. He called to Pua, "What's this?"

Pua went to the rear of the house, where Ulrich Schilling was, to see what he was talking about. She didn't see him come from behind the door when she walked into the master bedroom because his move was lightning fast. She might have, though, had it not been for being preoccupied by a text, from an interested buyer, that had just popped up on the screen of her phone. Schilling had the garrote around her neck, and he started to strangle her.

Unlike his other victims, Pua had been to the karate dojo a few times recently to brush up on her skills. When her muscle memory kicked in, she stomped his right foot and smashed her right fist into his groin, causing him to release the garrote around her neck. Pua was able to break free but had dropped her phone in the struggle. She was gasping for air and unable to continue to fight. Escape was her only option. She ran out of the house toward the barn at the edge of the coffee orchard, about a hundred yards away. Ulrich limped after her after he recovered enough from the pain she had inflicted on him. She ran inside the barn and hid, hoping Ulrich had not seen her go in–but he had.

Pua was hiding behind a row of pallets stacked five feet high with coffee beans. She had boxed herself in, realized her mistake and started to move when she heard the squeaky hinge of the barn door as Ulrich slowly pulled it open.

Her phone was still in the house. She had no choice but to

fight. Yelling for help wouldn't work since the property she was showing that day was a five acre coffee farm. The neighbors would never have heard her screams.

Just as Pua was getting up the nerve to face Ulrich, and fight for her life, they both heard a tractor coming back from the orchard. The barn door opened quickly and Ulrich disappeared into the orchard before the farm worker reached the barn.

Pua went back to the house and called 911. When the first responding officer arrived, she gave him a description of Ulrich. But unknown to them, he was wearing a wig. So the police were looking for a man with long blonde hair.

By that time Ulrich had already disposed of the wig and had doubled back to his car. He was long gone by the time other officers responded to the area.

After Pua called 911, she called Jessica. It took Jessica and Gabbie about ten minutes to get to Pua since the open house was up the mountain in Holualoa. When they got there, Jessica hugged Pua like she meant it, for the first time since their father's death. Jessica and Gabbie followed Pua back down the mountain to her office and checked her house, with their guns drawn, before allowing her to go inside. "Grab some clothes. You're coming to my house until we find this bastard," Jessica said. Pua packed a bag and thirty minutes later Gabbie took her to Sam and Jessica's, while Jessica drove straight to D&H Realty to look for Ulrich.

34

D&H REALTY

Jessica walked in the front door of D&H Realty and looked around the room. It was big and had a lot of desks separated by partitions forming little cubicles. She saw plenty of people in the room, but not Schilling. She glanced down at the receptionist sitting behind the counter. The young woman seemed to be doing her best to ignore Jessica while she talked on the phone and filed her nails.

"I'm looking for Ulrich Schilling, is he here?" Jessica asked the receptionist.

"I'm sorry, he's not available today. He's off island," she answered.

"Where did he go?"

"And you are?" the young woman asked.

Jessica parted the blazer she was wearing to show the receptionist her badge. When the young woman saw it, she changed her tune and answered the question. "He's in Honolulu today." Jessica handed the woman her card and said, "Please have him call me when he returns." She nodded she would, and Jessica thanked her and left.

The receptionist may have believed her boss had gone to Oahu, but Jessica didn't. It was no doubt a lie Ulrich had told his employee as an alibi. Jessica parked down the street from the real estate office to make some phone calls while she kept an eye on the place to see if Schilling would return. She called all the airlines that offered inter-island flights to Oahu. None of them had Ulrich Schilling on their passenger list.

Jessica went back to the real estate office to see the receptionist. "I have just one more question, are you sure he went to Honolulu because I can't find any record of him boarding a flight today," she said.

The snotty persona of the receptionist had returned when she said, "Of course not, he has his own plane." Jessica nodded and walked out the door.

***

After returning to the task force office, Jessica pulled out Ulrich Schilling's business card and dialed the number on it. Her repeated calls went straight to voicemail. After a couple hours with no response to the voicemails she had left, Jessica decided it was time to appeal to his sense of greed, to get him to come out in the open.

Jessica called Sam. "Hi honey, we can't wait for the Brew Fest. I need you to call Ulrich Schilling and tell him you want to see a house he has listed for sale in Kukio. Tell him you're getting ready to leave on a business trip and you would like to see the property before you go. Today or tomorrow, if possible."

"I thought you wanted to wait until the Brew Fest to try to get a DNA sample?"

"We can't. Somebody tried to strangle Pua earlier today. We think it was Schilling."

"Is she okay?" Sam asked. After Jessica assured him she was, he did as she had asked. Less than twenty minutes later his phone rang, and it was Ulrich Schilling returning his call.

"Aloha Mr. Stewart; you're interested in seeing the house I have listed in Kukio?" Schilling asked.

"Yes, that's right. I'm getting ready to leave on a business trip to Asia. I'll be there a couple weeks; but I'd really like to see the property before I go. I know its short notice. Would it be possible to see it either later this afternoon or tomorrow morning since I'm flying out tomorrow afternoon? I've been looking for a house in the Kukio Resort for a long time and this one is perfect. If I like it, I'm ready to write an offer."

The potential of a $20 million cash transaction was too much for Schilling to pass up. "We can see it any time because it's a vacation house and the sellers live on the mainland. How about this evening; we could meet at 5:30 p.m."

"Perfect. My wife and I will meet you then."

35

SAM AND JESSICA MEET

Sam and Jessica were early. He parked their Escalade in front of the house that was for sale in the Kukio Resort. Ulrich said they couldn't miss it because it had a pair of dolphin statues, one on each side at the entrance of the driveway.

Fifteen minutes later, a white late model BMW pulled up behind them and parked. Sam and Jessica got out of their vehicle and stood at the edge of the driveway, waiting for Schilling. Jessica noticed he had a slight limp.

The introductions were brief. Schilling began his sales pitch immediately. "There is koa wood throughout the house and you'll love the outdoor lava rock shower." Sam and Jessica nodded and acted like typical homebuyers, stopping to look at the koi pond before entering the house. Once at the front door, everyone kicked off their shoes before entering.

Ulrich was wearing loafers without socks, and Jessica looked at the top of his right foot and saw he had a large bruise there. She had looked for scratches on his neck when they first met at the driveway, but he wore a turtleneck shirt to the meeting and it covered them if there were any. A turtleneck in eighty-five degree weather in itself was suspicious.

"How did you get that nasty bruise on the top of your foot," she asked.

"Oh, one of my horses stepped on my foot by accident the other day when I startled it while it was at the trough eating. It was my fault for coming up from behind it," Schilling said, trying to make light of it.

"Good thing it didn't kick you in the balls too," she said nonchalantly as she looked at a six foot long blue marlin mounted on the living room wall.

The color drained from Schilling's face and he went from handsomely tanned to ghost white.

Jessica didn't miss a beat and continued with, "Nice sized living room. Does the furniture come with it?"

"It's negotiable," Schilling answered, his voice wavering.

By the time they had walked through the entire house, Jessica had asked enough questions that Sam was becoming concerned that she actually might want him to buy the house. He started giving her the side eye every time she asked another question about the place. It sounded like she was really interested in buying.

After they'd seen the house and started walking toward the driveway, Sam said, "We would like to make an offer."

"Great, follow me back to my office and we'll write it up."

"Excellent," Sam and Jessica answered at almost the same time.

Less than an hour later they were sitting in Schilling's office, back in Kona, at D&H Realty making small talk while Ulrich Schilling wrote the offer for twenty million dollars.

Sam put a contingency in the offer that they could back out within three days for any reason, since this was all a ruse to get Schilling's DNA.

Schilling wasn't happy about the clause, but he wrote the offer as Sam requested. Jessica had brought multiple swabs in her purse to check for DNA. They were ready to go but then she saw something she thought had Schilling's DNA on it. The hard part was going to be getting it without him noticing. The moment she was waiting for occurred when he set his eyeglasses down on the desk, while he went in the other room to make copies of the offer.

As soon as he left the room, Jessica pulled a swab out of her purse and rubbed the tip on the nose pads of his eyeglasses laying on top of his desk. As she spun the swab on the nose pad, it picked up the oily surface and got an excellent sample.

She had the second swab ready and quickly swabbed the edge of his coffee mug sitting on Ulrich's desk. She whispered to Sam, "Time for one more?" He nodded. The paper had jammed in the copier and he could see Schilling was trying to get it unstuck. Sam got up and stood in the doorway to block Schilling's view of Jessica gathering DNA samples. She quickly swabbed the brim of a hat sitting on a chair in the room's corner.

Jessica had put the swabs back in her purse just as Schilling returned from the copy machine. The three of them shook hands and Schilling promised to be in contact after he got a response from the seller. He stared at Sam and Jessica as they drove away. He knew she knew.

***

Sam and Jessica went to the task force office where Gabbie and O'Halleran were waiting to hear how it went.

"We got it," Jessica said as they walked in the office. O'Halleran and Gabbie high-five'd them.

"But the problem is we need to get the swabs to the FBI crime lab ASAP. We only have a three-day window to cancel the offer we made on a house we really don't want to own," Jessica said, with Sam nodding hard in agreement, a look of indigestion on his face.

O'Halleran said, "Let me make some phone calls." While

he was busy, Sam and Jessica gave Gabbie the play-by-play on how it went down. Ten minutes later O'Halleran got off the phone and said, "The fastest it will get there is FedEx, but that's going to be two days from now. We missed the cutoff for the flight tonight."

"Where exactly does it have to go?" Sam asked. Gabbie answered, "Virginia FBI crime lab." Sam nodded and said, "Let me make a phone call." He stepped outside and came back a couple minutes later. "I just had to make sure that my plane was ready; it just had a new engine installed. I wasn't sure if it was ready to go or not, but it is. I'll have the DNA delivered by tomorrow morning. All we have to do is drive it out to the airport and my pilots will leave tonight after they fuel and preflight the plane. You guys set it up so that somebody meets the plane at the airport in Virginia to transfer the DNA to the FBI."

"I can do that," Gabbie answered. She called a former colleague at the FBI and explained the situation. When she got off the phone, everyone was standing there waiting to hear what she had to say. "I had to call in a favor but I got it done."

"Good work guys," O'Halleran said as they all left the office. Sam and Jessica took the boxed up DNA evidence and drove it out to the airport. When they arrived at Air Services, they went into the office and Sam asked for a ride to the plane. The manager, Tim Elliott, was on duty that evening and was happy to oblige.

When they pulled up in front of the Gulfstream jet its navigation lights were on, the door was open, and the pilots were in the cockpit finishing the preflight. Sam carried the DNA evidence package up the staircase and stowed it in the closet. He stuck his head into the cockpit, "Thanks guys for making the last-minute trip."

Sam and Jessica sat in their vehicle and waited for the plane to take off before they left to go home. Fourteen minutes later the jet took off and made a climbing right turn out of Kona heading toward the U.S. mainland.

"By tomorrow morning when we wake up the package should be at the FBI lab," Sam said as he held Jessica's hand. They watched the plane disappear into the darkness.

36

DNA RESULTS

Sam and Jessica were expecting the DNA evidence to arrive the next morning in Virginia. But the new engine on the plane developed a problem five hours out of Kona and the captain diverted to Los Angeles. After a four-hour delay, and mechanics had repaired the problem, the DNA was back on its way to the FBI crime lab.

By the time the FBI received the evidence package, it was late afternoon. Usually the testing would have had to wait until the next day, but Gabbie pleaded with the lab to test the DNA that night. She explained it was from a serial killer case and the task force was afraid the suspect just might "rabbit." She promised to send them five pounds of Kona coffee and chocolate macadamia nuts for working overtime.

It was almost midnight when Gabbie got the test results back from the lab. Because of the time difference, it meant the FBI had worked through the night. The DNA from under Bonnie James' fingernails confirmed it was from Ulrich Schilling.

Gabbie called Jessica and gave her the news, and they made plans for arresting him in the morning.

Early the next day Sam called Ulrich and told him they

needed to meet because he was having second thoughts about the house they'd made an offer on. Ulrich agreed; he'd see them at his office later that morning at 9 a.m.

O'Halleran and Gabbie parked down the street and had D&H Realty under surveillance when Sam and Jessica rolled into the parking lot of the real estate office. Sam's first order of business was canceling the offer to buy the house in Kukio. Jessica sat quietly next to him in Ulrich's office while Sam told him the deal was off.

"May I ask why you're cancelling?" Ulrich questioned. "Because you're under arrest," Jessica answered.

Those were the magic words for O'Halleran and Gabbie to enter the office as backup. Jessica pulled her badge out of her pocket and held it in front of Ulrich so he could take a good look at it. "Put your hands behind your back and turn around," she ordered.

She couldn't remember the last time it felt so good to put the cuffs on someone as it did that morning.

They led Ulrich Schilling out of his office in handcuffs in front of all the real estate agents that worked there.

37

JUSTICE

They booked Ulrich Schilling into the Kona cellblock and gave him his one phone call. Like Clarence Valentine, he called high-profile criminal defense lawyer, Angela Reyes, in Honolulu. She told him the same thing she told Valentine when he called her from jail, "Don't say a word to anybody except me."

During his years of incarceration in a German prison he had studied American law and considered himself competent to act as his own lawyer, if he had to, but thought better of it for the time being.

The next day Schilling was taken to the Kona courthouse for his arraignment. His attorney was there waiting for him to arrive.

She and Schilling met before the arraignment to discuss the case and her fee. Schilling wasn't looking forward to a six figure legal bill, but he also didn't want to go to prison for the rest of his life either.

Schilling didn't think the DA could prove he was guilty beyond a shadow of a doubt. All the prosecution had was DNA. They had no other physical evidence, and they didn't have any witnesses.

He remembered the OJ Simpson trial and that OJ's lawyers had beat the DNA evidence. If they could do it, he reasoned he could do it too.

Now if he could make bail, that would be the issue of the day he most wanted to win.

Judge Tanaka read aloud in court that the state had charged Ulrich Schilling with first degree murder and asked him how he wanted to plead. "Not guilty, Your Honor," he answered.

The next order of business was the discussion of bail.

The district attorney, Carrie King, stood up and said, "Your Honor, we ask that the defendant be held without bond because he's a German national and a flight risk."

The defense attorney countered with, "My client is a local business owner and a pillar of the community. He has extensive real estate holdings that can be used for collateral and has a clean criminal record."

The DA shot back, "Mr. Schilling has a clean record here, but he did twenty years in a German prison for a murder, Your Honor."

The judge raised an eyebrow as he looked at the paperwork in front of him. He thought about it for a moment but sided with the prosecutor and said, "I agree with the state, Mr. Schilling will be held without bail." Schilling snapped the pencil he was holding and threw it down on the table, drawing a look of disapproval from the judge.

Angela Reyes got hired and fired all in the same day when she couldn't persuade the judge to release her client on bail. Schilling thought if she wasn't good enough to get him out on bail, she wouldn't be good enough to keep him from being convicted.

In the following weeks, Schilling told the court that he wanted to represent himself. The judge ruled that he was going to allow it, but would assign an attorney to assist Schilling in his defense.

Judge Tanaka also ruled Schilling didn't have to wear leg shackles or handcuffs while in the courthouse law library or when appearing in court.

Three Months Later.

One day when Schilling was locked in the law library at the courthouse, the sheriff's deputy guarding him stepped out of the room for a smoke break. While the deputy was out of the room, Schilling crawled out of the second floor window and escaped. When the deputy returned, he saw that Schilling was missing. He put out a broadcast that Ulrich Schilling had escaped from custody and the courthouse; the Kona PD searched the immediate area but came up empty.

Schilling had run down the hill from the courthouse to the highway and stuck his thumb out to catch a ride going north toward Kailua town.

Jessica and Gabbie heard over the police radio to be on the lookout for Ulrich Schilling, who had escaped from the courthouse ten minutes earlier. They were still on the job with the task force gathering evidence for Schilling's upcoming trial. They looked at each other and said, "Airport," at almost the same time. They grabbed their guns and ran out the door of the office. Jessica said, "You drive," as she pulled her phone out of her pocket.

They jumped into Gabbie's 4Runner and rushed to the airport while Jessica dialed Air Services and got Tim Elliot, the manager, on the phone.

"Tim, Jessica Kealoha here. I need you to keep Ulrich Schilling from taking his plane if he shows up at the airport. Slash its tires, park a fuel truck in front of it, I don't care what you have to do, but don't let that plane leave the ground. My partner and I are on the way."

Fifteen minutes later, Gabbie's truck screeched to a halt in front of the office at Air Services. Tim and Ulrich Schilling were sitting on the lanai out front. Tim had a .45 pointed at Schilling, and held it, until Jessica motioned for him to lower the weapon as they stepped up on the lanai.

Gabbie cuffed Schilling and put him in the 4Runner. Jessica looked at Tim and said, "You were just going to the gun range and stopped by the office to pick something up when I called you right?" as she nodded her head yes. "Yes, that's right," he answered and smiled. She thanked him for capturing Schilling and promised she and Sam would buy him dinner at Outback Steak House when this was all over.

Jessica and Gabbie took Schilling to the Kona cellblock to be put back in jail again. After that Jessica was going to call the sheriff to see about making sure Schilling didn't escape a second time.

38

TRIAL

Judge Tanaka rescinded his order, allowing Schilling to walk around without leg restraints and handcuffs. On the first day of his trial, he sat at the defense table with his court-appointed attorney who Judge Tanaka had assigned to assist. Schilling wore an expensive suit, his hair was neat, and he genuinely smiled when he looked toward the jury.

He didn't look like a serial killer. His real estate business had donated money to various charities and sports teams on the island, and he had a stellar reputation in the community. While the DNA evidence was compelling, it was a long way from being a done deal. He knew it, and the prosecutor knew it, too.

By the end of the first week of the trial, Jessica and Gabbie, who had sat in court watching the jury, took note of some jurors' body language. It was clear the prosecution was failing to convince them that Ulrich Schilling was guilty of murder.

That ringing shadow of doubt Jessica kept hearing in her head over and over was when Schilling said in court while addressing the jury, "Yes, the DNA was mine. But not because I murdered Bonnie James. It was because we had sex and she had dug her fingernails into my back, not because I strangled her. The only thing I'm guilty of is being in the wrong place at the wrong time."

At the lunch break Jessica and Gabbie went down the road a couple of miles to Teshima's for a couple bowls of saimin. Jessica dipped her spoon in the steaming bowl, scooped some noodles and blew on it before she said to Gabbie, "I'm starting to think Schilling could sell ice to an Eskimo." Gabbie nodded, "If we don't find the murder weapon we're going to lose this case. I can't fathom the thought of putting a serial killer back on the street." Jessica sighed and shook her head.

"We've been over his car, house and office. It's not there," Gabbie said. Jessica sighed again, her brows furrowed. They finished their lunch and went back to the courthouse. The DA was waiting for them in the hallway outside the courtroom. She motioned them away from the people nearby and said, "I need more evidence, we're losing. This thing's a coin toss right now. I'm considering offering him a plea deal if you guys don't come up with the murder weapon by the end of the trial tomorrow."

"We can see that. We'll go look again," Jessica said.

"Please get me something I can use to put this guy away," King said, just before she glanced at her watch. "Time for me to get back in there."

Jessica and Gabbie went back to the police impound yard to search Schilling's BMW again. They stood outside the car looking at it like a mountain they were about to climb. They searched the trunk and pulled the spare tire out. Gabbie opened the BMW tool kit wrapped in plastic and dumped out all the tools. Nothing.

Jessica pulled all the floor mats out of the car and put them on the roof. They popped the hood and looked in the engine compartment. There wasn't anything, not even a shop rag under the hood. They took some tools from the trunk and started taking parts off. First the front seats. Then the rear seat. They ripped the carpet out and only found seventy-five cents in change that had fallen under the back seat.

Two hours later, after looking in every nook and cranny they could to find the murder weapon, Jessica and Gabbie were exhausted. By then the BMW looked like it had been stolen and stripped for parts. Gabbie was sitting in the driver's seat, Jessica in the passenger. They had ripped the car apart and still hadn't found the garrote or a reasonable facsimile thereof.

Gabbie was the first one to speak after sitting there a few minutes. "I know this has nothing to do with this, but I got a recall notification from the dealer about my 4Runner. They want me to bring it in so they can install some filter under the dash that the factory failed to install for some weird reason. Have you ever heard of such a thing?"

Jessica slowly turned her head toward Gabbie and smiled. She then slowly turned back straight ahead and looked down at the open glove box that they had gone through at least ten times. She knew there wasn't anything in it and closed the door.

She slid out of the front seat and kneeled down alongside the open car door. She reached in and pulled off the bottom dash panel from underneath the glove box door, and when she did, the garrote fell on the floor. It was made with a stainless steel cord and had a wooden handle at each end. Simple and deadly.

"How did you know?" Gabbie shouted with excitement.

"This is how you get to the cabin air filter; that's the thing the dealer wants to install on your 4Runner. It's a relatively new feature on newer cars. I only learned about it the last time I took my car in for service, the mechanic said I needed one." Jessica pulled out her rubber gloves to pick up the murder weapon. "If it wasn't for you, I doubt I would have thought to look there."

Gabbie and Jessica stood back ten feet and took another

look at the Beemer they had turned into a bucket of bolts when Gabbie said, "Do you remember where all that stuff goes?" Jessica shook her head. "Maybe the high school auto shop would like a project car. Besides, I don't think Ulrich Schilling will be needing it anytime soon."

Jessica pulled her phone out of her back pocket and dialed the district attorney. She didn't answer. Jessica waited for the beep. "We found it. We're going to swab it for DNA as soon as we get back to the office. We'll bring the murder weapon to court in the morning."

39

RESULTS

Most mornings, before Sam and Jessica started their day, they sat out on the lanai and had a cup of coffee together while they watched the boats come and go from Keauhou Bay. He had just returned from a business trip to the mainland and was glad to be home. He longed for the day when she would retire again and could be with him wherever he had to go.

He also looked forward to the day when his back didn't hurt anymore. He'd tried everything but surgery, and found the only thing that seemed to work was hydrocodone. He had picked up a fresh supply of pain pills and had managed to reign in the urge to take more than four a day. He'd gone overboard with them a few times. He'd promised himself and Jessica he'd never take more than the daily maximum and so far had been able to stick to it.

Jessica was enjoying that particular morning more than any she could remember in a long time, as she sipped her coffee. All was right in her world. Sam asked, "How's the trial going?"

"It was a coin toss until yesterday when Gabbie and I found the murder weapon.

"No wonder you look so content this morning," Sam said as he smiled.

Jessica took another sip of coffee and said, "Between the shrink and catching Schilling, I think I'm finally starting to get some peace in my life. I think the murder weapon we found will connect him to most of the other murders except for Pam Gorky. He probably used something different to strangle her with and if he didn't, the DNA would have been washed away. And I doubt we'll ever find the other murder weapon if there was one. We just have to wait until the DNA results from the garrote come back."

Jessica took the last sip of her coffee, stood and stretched. "I have to get ready for court."

Sam stood up and wrapped his arms around her and she put hers around him. "After this is over, I think we should get in our canoe, paddle across the bay to the church at the resort and tie the knot," Sam whispered in her ear.

Jessica tilted her head back from his shoulder and said, "Are you sure that's what you want to do? The shrink hasn't exactly said I'm not crazy," she winked.

"I'm sure." Sam kissed her softly as he held her tight for a moment, not wanting to let go.

***

Jessica and Gabbie shipped the DNA swabs to the FBI lab first thing that morning before going to the courthouse.

"Even if we don't get a hit on the DNA from the victim and we don't get a conviction on any of the other murders, there's an excellent chance he will get nailed for the Bonnie James murder," Jessica said as they drove away from the UPS store.

Fifteen minutes before the trial was to resume, Jessica and Gabbie met district attorney Carrie King in the hallway outside the courtroom. "Merry Christmas," Jessica said as she handed her a paper bag containing the murder weapon and followed her into the courtroom.

Ulrich Schilling sat at the defendant's table, joking with the attorney assigned to assist him in his defense. Schilling looked like a player sitting on the bench of a winning football team as the clock counted down the last ten seconds of the game.

"All rise," the bailiff said as Judge Tanaka entered the courtroom. Jessica and Gabbie sat behind the prosecutor. Jessica whispered to Gabbie, "I can't wait to see the look on that smug bastard's face when he finds out we have the murder weapon." Gabbie smiled and nodded.

When it was time to get started Carrie King said, "Your Honor, the state would like to introduce new evidence that has come to light." She reached into the paper bag and pulled the garrote out of it. There were gasps heard coming from the other side of the courtroom where Schilling's supporters sat. Most of them were real estate agents from his firm.

Jessica was looking straight at Schilling. Just as she expected, when the prosecutor pulled the murder weapon from the bag it wiped the smile right off of Schilling's face. This time Jessica wore the smug smile from the satisfaction of a job well done.

Ulrich Schilling jumped up and said, "I object! This is the first time I've heard of any new evidence Your Honor." Judge Tanaka looked at Carrie King who was still standing. "Your Honor, I just received the murder weapon moments before coming into the courtroom."

"Overruled. I'll allow it," Judge Tanaka said.

Carrie King handed the bag with the murder weapon in it to the bailiff. Jessica and Gabbie looked over at the jury and could see by the looks on their faces that the tide had turned in the prosecution's favor.

Gabbie whispered to Jessica as she looked back from the jury. "Those are the looks jurors have when they are sending someone to prison." Jessica nodded and smiled.

The following day the jury heard closing arguments.

Instead of denying the garrote was his, Ulrich Schilling told the jury he and Bonnie James were playing a kinky sex game that accidentally went too far; her death had been a tragic accident.

The jury didn't buy it. When they came back from deliberations the next day, they found him guilty of murder in the first degree.

When the DNA tests returned from the FBI lab a week later, the findings showed there was a hodgepodge of DNA from multiple victims on the stainless steel cord and the wooden handles. Pua's was found there too. The icing on the cake was Schilling's DNA being present on the wood handles.

Over the course of the next six months, the state tried and convicted Ulrich Schilling on multiple murder charges for the real estate brokers he had strangled.

The jury came back with a unanimous decision in each of those cases. They convicted Schilling of murder and sentenced him to life in prison plus a hundred and twenty years. Jessica felt real peace for the first time knowing that Ulrich Schilling would spend the rest of his life in an Arizona prison, where Hawaii sent a lot of their most violent criminals.

40

MISSING PERSONS

A new custom home subdivision and ocean front golf course was being built on top of a large lava flow just north of town. Bulldozers and excavators had worked all over the lava field, getting it prepared, before the building of homes could start. Construction came to a halt on the third day when a bulldozer fell into a lava tube below the surface.

Over thousands of years, lava tubes had formed all over the west side of the island. It was not unheard of for a heavy piece of construction equipment to break through the lava and fall into a tube. But this time was different.

The bulldozer operator was uninjured and climbed down off of it. As he looked around the dozer it was surrounded by bones. Finding bones in lava tubes was not uncommon. But finding fully dressed skeletons was.

Jessica got off the phone and turned to Gabbie. "We have to go take a look at a lava tube where that new housing development is going in, out by the harbor."

Gabbie looked confused for a moment and finally said, "Lava tube?"

"It's full of bones–human bones," Jessica said as she picked up her purse.

"Are we talking something like the Thurston lava tube at the volcano?" Gabbie asked, as they headed out the door of the office.

"It could be. But I've never seen one that big. But, if it's big enough to swallow a bulldozer, it's pretty darn big, no matter what."

***

The roof of the lava tube was only a few feet from the surface. It would support the weight of people and light vehicles, but the bulldozer was too much. On the first pass over that part of the property its weight caused the ground to open up and swallow the dozer like a sink hole.

The construction crew had found an entrance to the tube a few hundred yards from where the dozer had broken through the roof of the tube. When they followed the tube from the newly created sink hole they found the secret entrance. It had been missed during the land survey. Brush from a nearby kiawe tree had been piled over the entrance to hide it.

"Now I see why they called us and not the burial council," Jessica said, as she and Gabbie stared at the skeletons neatly laid side by side, fully dressed in clothes from the last twenty years.

Gabbie knelt down to take a closer look at one of the fifteen skeletons; it still was wearing a yellow mini-skirt. "I remember one of the missing persons reports saying the victim was wearing a yellow skirt when she disappeared," Gabbie said.

"I think we just found the lair of whomever is responsible for the missing women from the cold cases," Jessica said, as she knelt down on the other side of the victim.

As the sunlight shone into the lava tube it reflected off a metallic object twenty feet away and caught Jessica's attention. "Look," she said, and pointed toward the reflection of the gun.

It was another skeleton, but it was different from all the

others. This one wore Levi's and work boots, with an auto mechanic style work shirt. The object that caught Jessica's eye was a nickel plated pistol, lying beside the skeleton.

"Maybe the guilt got to him," Gabbie said, as she and Jessica examined the bullet hole in the side of the skull.

***

A month later, when the lab results came back from the skeletons' DNA, the results confirmed they were all female with the exception of the one that had a bullet hole in the skull. Every one of the women reported missing, over the previous twenty years, was found in the lava tube, plus a few that weren't reported. Those were most likely homeless women that nobody had missed.

It became clear to Jessica why the mayor overreacted, a couple of months earlier at their meeting, when she mentioned the missing persons cold cases. One of the skeletons found was a cousin of his, who was a known prostitute on the Hilo side of the island.

O'Halleran compared the DNA of the skeleton with the bullet hole to DNA found on one of the victims on Oahu–it was a match. After further investigation, O'Halleran discovered a shop owner by the name of Robert Trawler, who lived in Hilo, was the skeleton with the bullet hole. Trawler owned three automotive transmission shops, one in Hilo, one in Kona and one in Honolulu and traveled between the three every week. O'Halleran had been on to him in Honolulu but could never prove his involvement until now.

41

WEDDING

SIX MONTHS LATER.

The small chapel on the grounds of the Keauhou Bay Resort overlooked the Pacific Ocean and Keauhou Bay. Over a hundred of Sam and Jessica's friends and family filled it to capacity.

Sam stood with his best man, Uncle Frank, and the minister. Sam wore a traditional lei, made from green maile leaves interwoven with white tuberose flowers, over his cream colored Tommy Bahama shirt and matching slacks.

When The Hawaiian Wedding song began to play, Jessica entered the back of the church with Uncle Jack, who she asked to walk her down the aisle. Henry was in front of them throwing red and white plumeria flowers.

Jessica wore a champagne and ivory colored, open back V-neck dress by Kleinfeld. She had a white plumeria flower over her right ear and a ginger lei. All eyes were on her as she glided down the aisle to stand next to Sam.

Uncle Jack and Henry took a seat, and the minister began the ceremony. When he got to the part where he asked if anyone had an objection, Jessica whispered to Sam, "I have a Glock in a leg holster under this dress if anyone thinks they're going to ruin my wedding." She smiled, but Sam wondered if she really was packing.

By the end of the ceremony, they both had tears in their eyes from the overwhelming emotion of their lifelong commitment to each other. Afterward, Jessica whispered to Sam as they walked out of the chapel, "Now you're legally mine."

They held the reception on the lush tropical grounds next to the chapel. The catering department of the hotel had set up a seafood buffet and an open bar. A Hawaiian trio provided the live entertainment; one played slack key guitar, the other, a twelve string guitar as a hula dancer performed while they played.

Sam's best man, Uncle Frank, had flown in from Las Vegas. He stood outside the chapel sizing up the crowd for damsels in distress, while he and Uncle Jack smoked cigars and compared war stories of weddings past.

Pua was buzzing around the courtyard visiting with guests from out of town, when Jessica pulled her aside for a moment and said, "I love you. Thank you for all of the hard work you put into helping me get ready this morning," and she handed her a jewelry box.

Pua was Jessica's maid of honor, something neither of them would have ever thought possible before. Their relationship the previous six months had become closer than it had ever been. Pua was instrumental in helping Jessica plan and get ready for the wedding. The jewelry box contained a gold bracelet with the inscription on the inside that said, "Sisters forever. I love you and I'll always have your back–Jess."

While people ate, Sam and Jessica made the rounds from one table to the next, thanking aunties and uncles who had flown in from all over to attend, or driven from across town.

Two hours later, after lots of photos and the cutting of the wedding cake, everyone in the immediate family and the wedding party sat at a large table reminiscing about the good times and some bad.

When the musicians began to perform the song Hanalei Moon, the crowd became quiet. Sam and Jessica got up from their table and had their first dance.

After they returned to their table, Uncle Jack came over and sat next to Jessica. "You look beautiful. I know your mother and father would be proud if they were here," he said, as he glanced over at the table that had her and Sam's parents' photos displayed with a lit candle. Her eyes welled with tears as she nodded. Uncle Jack gave her a firm hug with one arm around her shoulder before getting up to get another drink.

After he left the table, Gabbie came over and sat by Jessica. "Ulrich Schilling should be on his way to an Arizona prison right about now," she said. That snapped Jessica back into the present.

"Hallelujah. I'm glad that chapter in our lives is over. Maybe now we can get back to going to the beach," she answered.

"I'm looking forward to going fishing. Not the two legged kind either," Gabbie said, as she watched Uncle Frank coming toward the table.

Jessica whispered, "I wouldn't turn my nose up at that, he's pretty wealthy from what I hear, I think he owns a casino in Laughlin, Nevada."

Gabbie shook her head and whispered back, "I don't care about the money, my pension from the FBI is just fine, besides, he's too old for me. I plan on being a cougar from now on. I need me a cub that I can raise right," she winked.

Sam shifted his chair closer to Jessica so Uncle Frank could sit down. He had struck out finding any damsels in distress that needed saving, and decided to give it a rest and join the conversation. He asked Sam, "Where do people that live in Hawaii go to honeymoon?"

"New Zealand, we love it there. Now that Jessica has retired again, we plan to visit at least once a year from now on."

It was late afternoon, near time for sunset, and the sky was crystal clear. Everyone stood at the edge of the bay watching as the big red ball sunk below the horizon, hoping to see if there would be a green flash. After the usual disagreements as to whether or not there was such a thing, Sam said to the group, "It's time my beautiful bride and I wish everyone aloha since we fly out early in the morning."

They waved to the crowd of friends and family still gathered on the shoreline. Sam and Jessica climbed into their canoe and paddled across the bay to their home.

42

HONEYMOON

The next morning before Sam and Jessica left on their honeymoon, Auntie May stopped by. She had come to pick up Henry to stay with her ohana while they were away in New Zealand. Her six boys, who ranged in age from six to fifteen, would keep Henry plenty busy while Sam and Jessica were away.

"I almost feel jealous," Jessica said as she and Sam watched Henry drive away with Auntie May. She shook her head and continued, "Have you ever noticed he never cries when he leaves with her." Sam nodded. "Yup, there's something just not fun about us I guess," he joked, as they strolled back in the house to make final preparations and lock it up before Gabbie arrived to take them to the airport.

Jessica's phone buzzed in her pocket. It was Gabbie. She had sent a text, and it said, *"I'm on my way. I overslept, I'll be there in ten."* Jessica texted her back, *"No worries,"* and hollered to Sam in the back bedroom that Gabbie was running late.

"Does that mean we have time for a quickie?" he yelled back.

"You wish, lover boy. I'll pull the Escalade out of the garage."

All the suitcases were in the Cadillac and Jessica was leaning against the side of it when Gabbie showed up eight minutes later. She looked disheveled but had a glow about her. "Rough night?" Jessica asked, while waiting for Sam to finish locking the house.

Gabbie grinned before she answered. "I might have to change my thinking about older men. He had snow on the roof, but there was definitely a fire in the furnace."

Gabbie had brought a bottle of white shoe polish with her. After Sam and Jessica were inside the Cadillac, she scribbled on the back of it, "*Just Married,*" before leaving for the airport. People honked and waved shakas as Sam and Jessica drove down the highway to the airport.

When Gabbie pulled up in front of Air Services, the staff quickly transferred the luggage from the Escalade to their plane. Gabbie hugged Sam and Jessica before they got into the shuttle that would take them through the controlled gate to the waiting jet.

***

It was a busy morning at the Kona airport for both commercial and private planes. The inter-island Hawaiian Airlines jets were coming and going and there were at least a dozen Gulfstream private planes parked on the ramp.

Jessica could never tell which plane was theirs, they all looked alike to her except for the one owned by the Cirque du Soleil guy. His jet's paint changed colors when she looked at it as they passed by in the shuttle.

Sam had seen to it that Jessica would never again have to wonder about his loyalty. He'd had her name painted on the side of their plane, in two foot high letters using a translucent paint that was the same base color as her two birthstones, peridot and spinel.

The flight crew stood at the door and congratulated Sam

and Jessica as they boarded the Gulfstream jet. "Mr. and Mrs. Stewart, we'll be departing for Christchurch in just a couple of minutes," the captain said.

After stowing their carry-ons, Sam and Jessica got settled in for the nine hour flight to New Zealand. She looked forward to the long flight so she could catch up on her sleep. It had been in short supply the previous month leading up to the wedding because of all the planning involved.

Minutes later as the plane accelerated down the runway she glanced out the window, looking at Mount Hualalai as the plane lifted off the runway. It was a beautiful morning. The sky was postcard blue and the turquoise–hued water below became visible from her side of the plane, as it climbed out over the ocean heading south away from the island. It was mesmerizing watching fishing boats leaving the harbor as they headed for the fishing grounds in search of thousand pound blue marlins. It always reminded her of the times she and her father had fished together.

She sunk into the soft leather recliner and relaxed. Twenty minutes out of Kona she was almost asleep when her phone starting ringing. It jolted her awake.

"Hello."

"This is the U.S. Marshals' office in Las Vegas, Nevada. We were told to notify you that Ulrich Schilling escaped coming off the plane from Hawaii."

Jessica went from almost asleep to wanting to throw her phone against the bulkhead. She took a deep breath, exhaled and asked, "When?"

"This morning," the deputy said.

"Thanks." She put the phone down and looked over at Sam. "How would you like to go to Las Vegas instead?

THE END

ALSO BY J.E. TRENT

Prequel to book 1. Death in Hawaii Get this prequel for free when you join my email list. It's the only place it's available.- **Click here.**

Hawaii Thriller Series

Book 1 Death in Paradise

Book 2 Death Orchid

ABOUT THE AUTHOR

J.E. Trent

J.E. Trent is an emerging author of Hawaii crime thrillers. The Hawaii Thriller Series takes place on the Kona side of the big island of Hawaii.

J.E. Trent lived full time in Hawaii for over twenty two years and loves sharing his knowledge of the tropical paradise in his novels.

Hawi
Honokaa
Waimea
Mauna Kea
Hilo
Kona
Hawaii
Pahoa
Mountain
View
Captain
Cook
Mauna Loa
Pahala
Naalehu

Kauai
Kekaha
Kapaa
Lihue
Puuwai
Niihau
PACIFIC OCEAN
Oahu
Pearl City
Honolulu
Molokai
Kaunakakai
Maui
Wailuku
Hana
Lanai
Kahoolawe
Hawi
Honokaa
Waimea
Hilo
Kailua
Hawaii
Pahoa
Captain Cook
Mountain View
Pahala
Naalehu
HAWAII

ACKNOWLEDGMENTS

A Big Mahalo to Judith Shaw and my wife, Eila, for the final edit. It was only because of their input that this story came out as well as it did. I'm truly blessed to have her kokua. (help)

Shane Rutherford at Dark Moon Graphics made the beautiful cover for the book.

Mahalo to all the authors who have shared their knowledge at kboards.com and the 20BooksTo50K Facebook group and many others.

Mahalo to my friend Capt. Steve Kaiser who has taken me deep sea fishing aboard his Cabo many times. I am indebted to him for sharing his in-depth knowledge of the sea with me. He has been a great friend for over twenty years and for that, I'm a very grateful.

Mahalo to my friend John Masters for sharing his knowledge of deep sea fishing with me over lunch. The mere mention of his name in Hawaiian waters makes fish tremble.

He's living proof you don't need a big boat, it's what you do with your pole that matters.

AFTERWORD

At the time when I got the idea for Sam and Jessica I had been an auto mechanic for about thirty-five years. I was over fifty and my body was screaming at me every morning that I'd better find another way to make a living. Around that time I had written some flash fiction that I had gotten a lot of positive feedback on and thought with some study that maybe I could write a novel.

After a lot of brainstorming, Sam and Jessica came to be. A billionaire super yacht builder and a retired LA detective. They aren't perfect; they're growing through problems in their lives that people can relate to. They have character defects just like everybody does. But it's how they strive to overcome them and do the right thing, is what I hope to convey in their stories going forward in the Death in Hawaii Series.

During the twenty-two years I lived on the big island, I witnessed some amazing things. Those events are where a lot of the inspiration I get comes from. My goal is to intersperse those moments in my books creating something unique that you can only get when you read my stories.

Hawaii is a magical place, my words will never do it justice. I hope that readers of the Death in Hawaii series take away a bit of aloha after spending time with Sam and Jessica.

Get the free prequel and new release notifications.

https://readerlinks.com/l/965413

HAWAIIAN GLOSSARY

Mana (Ma-Na)

Spirit

Aina (Eye-Na)

Land of the island.

Beach Boys

They light the resort's tiki torches, pull the pig from the imu and help tourists safely enjoy the beach.

Honu (Ho-Nu)

It is a green sea turtle.

Malama (Ma-La-ma)

To take care of.

Hapa (Ha-Pa)

Means mixed race. Hawaiian, Chinese, Japanese, Portuguese and Filipino make up the majority of the population in Hawaii and when they marry their children are called hapa. A mixture.

Huli-huli chicken is grilled on a trailer in a parking lot or on the side of the road. It's usually related to a fundraiser.

Da-Kine (dah-KINE) is a fill in word used for anything you can't remember the name of.

Aloha (ah-LOH-hah)

Aloha is "hello" and "goodbye." You could also have the spirit of aloha = Giving, caring.

Mahalo (mah-HA-loh)

Means "thank you."

Haole (HOW-leh)

It's used to refer to white people. It can be used offensively, but isn't always meant to be insulting. Originally it meant foreigner, but I seriously doubt anyone uses it for that anymore.

Kane (KAH-neh)

Kane refers to men or boys.

Wahine (wah-HEE-neh)

Wahine refers to women or girls.

Keiki (KAY-kee)

This word means "child." You may hear locals call their children "keiki."

Hale (HAH-leh)

Hale translates to "home" or "house." It can often refer to housing in general.

Pau (POW)

When you put the soy sauce bottle down, you may hear a local ask, "Are you pau with that?" Pau essentially means "finished" or "done."

Howzit (HOW-zit)

In Hawaii, "howzit" is a common pidgin greeting that translates to "hello" or "how are you?"

Lolo (loh-loh)

When someone calls you "lolo," they're saying you're "crazy or dumb." It's sometimes used in a teasing manner.

Ono (OH-noh)

Ono means "delicious." It can often be paired with the pidgin word "grinds," which translates to "food." So, if you eat something delicious, you might say it's ono grinds.

Ohana (oh-HAH-nah)

Means family.

Tita (tit-uh)

Refers to a woman or teenage girl who could be said to either be a tomboy or else somewhat aggressive, tough, or rough with her language or manners.

Tutu (too-too)

Means grand mother. Google says it references both grand parents, but I've never heard that on the island.

BOATING GLOSSARY

Saloon = Living room. The social area of a larger boat is called the *saloon*. However, it is pronounced "salon."

Cockpit = Is a name for the location of controls of a vessel; while traditionally an open well in the deck of a boat outside any deckhouse or cabin, in modern boats they may refer to an enclosed area.

Head = Is the bathroom.

Galley = Kitchen.

Stateroom = Bedroom.

Bulkhead = Wall.

Line = Rope.

Port = Standing at the rear of a boat and looking forward, "port" refers to the entire left side of the boat.

Starboard = Standing at the rear of a boat and looking forward, "starboard" refers to the entire right side of the boat.

B.O.A.T. = Bust Out Another Thousand$

COPYRIGHT

This book is a work of fiction created by J.E. Trent.

Lightning Source UK Ltd.
Milton Keynes UK
UKHW010657300522
403720UK00002B/213